STUDENT NURSE

STUDENT NURSE

GAIL JORDAN

CUTTING EDGE

ISBN-13: 978-1-962896-39-9

Published by
Cutting Edge Books
PO Box 8212
Calabasas, CA 91372
www.cuttingedgebooks.com

TABLE OF CONTENTS

CHAPTER ONE

"THEM AS HAS GITS!"

THE VERY PRETTY girl in the blue-gray uniform beneath an immaculate white apron, her flame-colored hair uncapped, came briskly into the living room. Her brown-gold eyes were merry, her mouth curled in a professionally bright smile.

"Good morning," she said cheerfully.

The short, stocky man who might have been anywhere from thirty-five to sixty (as a matter of fact he was forty-two) all but glared at her as he placed himself defensively against the bedroom door.

"What's good about it?" he growled. "Damned birds yackety-yacking since before daylight and the whole place crawling with quiet. Gimme Broadway any time."

The girl chuckled and moved toward the door, carrying the small tray carefully in her two hands.

"I'd love to," she told him with that little smile that made him hate her. "But this happens to be the Happy Valley Nursing Home."

"Happy Valley my—" The man barely managed to swallow the obscene word and went on hastily. "You can't come in here. The boss don't wanna see you."

"That's too bad." The girl seemed properly regretful. "But I'm afraid he hasn't much to say about whom he sees or doesn't see. I have orders to see that he drinks this."

The short, stocky man reached for a tray.

"Gimme it; I'll see he gets it."

The girl swung the tray neatly out of his reach.

"Sorry. I have to give it to him personally," she said.

The ugly man drew his brows together in an unpleasant frown.

"Look, why don't you dames leave the boss alone? So all right, he's got a private key to the mint; sure, he's good-looking and got what it takes to get all you dames hot and bothered; but I'm tellin' you you ain't goin' in!"

The pretty girl eyed him for a moment, and then she put the tray down on a small table and faced him, cool-eyed, quiet-voiced.

"Get away from that door!" she ordered authoritatively.

Beelzy's small, close-set eyes blazed.

"Look who's givin orders."

"I'm not giving them, I'm following them," she corrected him curtly. "Doctor's orders. Your boss is a patient here and while he's here, he'll do what he's told. And so will you."

Beelzy took a step toward her, his eyes vicious.

"Scram, cutie," he ordered, and reached for her.

The next moment, to his amazement, he was lying flat on his back halfway across the room, and the girl, completely unruffled, picked up the tray and went into the bedroom and closed the door quietly behind her.

The girl smiled serenely at the tall, blond young man with a dark silk robe belted snugly about him. "Good morning, Mr. Ainslee. Your eggnog—and I have to take your temperature," she said cheerfully.

Jordan Ainslee stared at her, his blue eyes wide.

"What happened to Beelzy? he asked.

The girl looked momentarily embarrassed.

"I'm sorry," she said as though she meant it. "He didn't want me to come in, and I had orders, so—" She lifted her shoulders in a little shrug.

"I heard that," said Jordan, still eyeing her sharply. "And following that I heard a dull thud. Could that have been Beelzy?"

The girl flushed to the roots of her flame-red hair and her eyes dropped from Jordan's stunned regard.

"I'm afraid so," she admitted reluctantly.

"What did you hit him with, a baseball bat?"

"Of course not! It—well, it was judo," she told him.

Jordan said something under his breath. It could have been an oath or it could have been a prayer. She could take her choice. Jordan's fascinated eyes took her in from the top of her flaming hair, which was tucked into a neat coiffure that tried unsuccessfully to deny its deep natural waves, to the tip of her sensible white rubber-soled nurse's shoes.

"Judo!" he murmured in a tone of wonder.

Still flushed and uncomfortable, the girl explained awkwardly. "My father was born in Japan, the son of missionaries in a remote mission. He became interested in judo as a boy, and became very expert. He was an instructor here for years at one of the military schools; he began teaching me when I was five. It—well, it comes in handy sometimes."

Jordan was still staring at her as though she were some strange creature the like of which he had never seen before, and his blue eyes, creeping over her, dwelled a little hungrily on the charms the blue-gray chambray of her crisp uniform defined rather than concealed.

"And now," said the girl hurriedly, still avoiding his eyes, "your eggnog."

Jordan shuddered as she lifted the glass from the tray.

"Eggnog!" he shuddered, his handsome mouth curling with distaste. "It's blasphemy to call a concoction like this 'eggnog.' I bet there isn't a drop of alcohol in it."

"Of course not," the girl agreed serenely. "But you must drink it—doctor's orders."

"Why?"

"I wouldn't know," she agreed frankly. "I don't ask questions — I just obey orders."

The door behind her opened and Beelzy stood there, his eyes blazing with wrath and amazed disbelief as he stared at the girl.

"Boss, she slugged me!" he gasped.

"I know," said Jordan, and sipped with a wry look at the eggnog. "Judo, my boy."

Beelzy gasped, and his eyes widened.

"Judo? *Her?*" He jerked a thumb at her in shocked amazement. "A broad that knows judo? What's the world comin' to?"

"I'm sorry," the girl apologized sincerely. "But you were in my way."

"Boss, what chance has a guy got when the dames start after him using judo?" Beelzy was ignoring her. "You might as well give up."

Jordan grinned, his blue eyes filled with admiration and quickening interest.

"I think you've got a point there, Beelzy," he admitted. "And somehow the thought of surrender is rather appealing."

Beelzy gave a little shocked cry of protest.

"Boss! I was only kiddin'. Don't encourage her. Remember what a time we had gettin' loose from the last tomato you talked to like that?"

The girl stared from Beelzy to Jordan, and her own eyes were wide and shocked.

"For heaven's sake!" she protested, amused and resentful at the same time. "You two idiots don't think—oh, my goodness! I'm not making a play for your boss, Beelzy. What a silly idea!"

Beelzy said sharply. "Oh. it is, is it? Well, there's been a lot of dames didn't think so."

"And what, may I ask," protested Jordan, his voice overriding Beelzy's angry whine, "is so silly about a dame—I mean a girl—making a play for me?"

The girl flushed a little but met his eyes straightly.

"I don't mean to be insulting, Mr. Ainslee." she said quietly. "You are young, handsome, charming, and rich; but to me. you're just a patient and I'm a nurse. Not even a real honest to goodness nurse; I'm just a probationer. But if I'm good and study hard and work my head off. then I'll be a student nurse and some day a R.N. And that's what interests me—not the patients who come along in my day's work."

Jordan stared at her lovely, earnest young face, but before he could speak Beelzy burst into furious speech. "Playin' hard to get, eh? Well, you're wastin' your time, baby. The boss don't fall for none o' that stuff."

"Shut up, Beelzy, or I'll sic her on you again," ordered Jordan, still without taking his eyes off the girl. "How about having dinner with me tonight?"

The girl laughed outright.

"In the first place, it wouldn't be permitted," she began.

"Oh, it wouldn't? See here, I'm a patient here—not a prisoner."

"And anyway, my aunts wouldn't allow me to date a patient, even if the hospital would," she told him coolly. She picked up the tray, put on it the glass he had emptied almost without being conscious of it, and turned to the door.

"Here, wait a minute. Why, I don't even know your name," protested Jordan. He reached the door ahead of her and held it shut, while he stood looking down at her, his blue eyes dark with curiosity and interest."What's your name?" he repeated.

"I'm Martha Desmond," she told him.

"Will I see you again?" he asked anxiously.

"No doubt; I work here." With that she turned the knob and drew the door shut behind her.

For a long moment after the door closed, Jordan stood still, staring at it. And Beelzy, watching him like an anxious mother hen, groaned a little.

"Hold on to your hats, boys; here we go again!" he groaned, and hid his face behind his calloused hands.

Without looking at him, Jordan spoke curtly over his shoulder.

"Find out whether there's a decent place for dining within a fifty-mile radius," he ordered crisply. "And tell the doctor I want to see him at once."

Beelzy grinned wryly.

"You ain't been yourself the coupla weeks you have been here, boss," he said dryly. "You don't send for the saw-bones around here; they drop in to see you whenever it suits them. Oh, sure, you're paying a coupla hundred bucks a week for the cottage and all the 'with-its,' but just the same, they look in when they feel like it—not when you want 'em to. They got regular hours. Be one around here at twelve o'clock. Then again at four, but it won't be the same one. I dunno—they kinda divide up a patient, set him off in sections. The twelve o'clock one checks you from hairpins to collarbuttons; the one comes at four takes over from there and works down."

"Stop yammering and find out about a place where I can take Martha to dinner," ordered Jordan sharply.

Beelzy stared at him, wide-eyed, and then his thick shoulders drooped and he plodded toward the door.

'Martha' yet," he muttered to himself, careful that his voice did not quite reach Jordan. " 'Martha' five minutes after he looks at her. Tomorrow it will be 'Honey Lamb' and a coupla days later she'll lower the boom on him and it'll cost us dough to get rid of her. Damned little twist! I oughta wring her neck."

But if Jordan heard, he said nothing. And his eyes were so intent, his manner so absorbed that it is likely his ears were closed to anything but the remembered sound of Martha's voice that had been pleasantly deep and warm, almost a little throaty. The kind of voice Jordan liked very much in a woman. And girls with that shade of red hair, and eyes that were golden-brown—how long had it been since he had known a girl with that coloring? Genuine, that is? She was so young and fresh and virginal—virginal? His mind tripped a little on that word and he considered it long and thoughtfully before he nodded and accepted it. Yes, he thought it might be quite likely. After all, she was not more than nineteen or twenty at the most, and if she had come straight here from high school to begin her training... Still, high-school kids were supposed to be pretty wise about sex nowadays; according to the Kinsey report, many of them began their "sex education" at the incredible age of thirteen, fourteen, or fifteen. But remembering the candid eyes, the way the girl had looked at him so directly, he was a little inclined to believe that she might, after all, be completely innocent. The thought packed a wallop...

Jordan Ainslee had been born to a great fortune, invested in such a way that no matter what he did, it went on growing and increasing. He could do whatever he wanted with the staggering annual income, but he could not touch the investments and the trust funds and the principal. Not that he had ever wanted to, for business bored him terrifically. He was interested in living, with a capital L. And for Jordan, Living meant show business. To the surprise of many, he had a distinct flair shown for acting and producing, and since he could (and did) bank-roll his own productions, he was always in supreme authority. Now and then he produced something that was a hit. He was smart enough to fight somewhat shy of the "arty" type of production, the tragedies, the "experimental" type. Ainslee Productions were usually lavish and girly musicals, revues, smart drawing-room comedies, and just occasionally a good, sound dramatic show with general appeal.

Other producers who had to have "angels" to provide their backing and usually had to be burdened with some angel's girl friend in return for necessary backing, looked sourly at the box-office hits with which Jordan occasionally came up and growled, "Them as has, *gits!*" And they hated him cordially and imitated him slavishly as far as they could.

But Beelzy, who had once been a ver ysmall-time prizefighter Jordan had owned and managed, knew that there was just one thing that really interested Jordan seriously. And that, in Beelzy's language, was "dames, broads, tomatoes, bimbos and babes." In his own brand of language, each word meant something special. He had classified them all; he boasted he could look at "something in skirts" and tell within minutes in which classification she belonged. But whatever her classification, she always meant "Trouble" to Beelzy. So now as he departed to follow the boss' orders, he wished savagely that he'd kicked the little nurse out of the joint the first time he set eyes on her.

CHAPTER TWO

CONCEPT OF MORALS

"Y OU'RE LATE, CHILD," protested aunt Elizabeth as she opened the door of the neat little cottage when she heard the sound of the old jalopy in the drive. "Come in out of the cold; you'll catch your death."

Martha, in the worn red coat that swore furiously at her hair and eyes but that was comfortingly warm, laughed as she ran along the neat brick walk between dead stalks of what had been Aunt Arleen's prized perennials last summer and into the house.

She dropped a light kiss on Aunt Elizabeth's cheek and dropped her coat gratefully.

"Umm—something smells good." She sniffed with appreciation.

"Arleen's making lamb stew with dumplings," said Elizabeth. "It's the fifteenth of the month."

"Oh, so it is—payday! Grandad's stock pays off."

"Your grandfather was very anxious that Arleen and I should never have to accept charity in our old age and arranged for us to have a small income," said Elizabeth. And Martha, who had heard countless times of Grandad's providence, nodded happily.

"And when I finish my training and get to be an R.N. making loads of money, you and Aunt Arleen shall have lamb stew with dumplings every night in the week," she promised gaily.

"We'd probably get very tired of it, don't you think? Are you still happy in your chosen career, child?"

"I'm the most lowly thing a hospital ever saw, darling—a probationer," laughed Martha. "But I do like it and I'm determined to be a really fine nurse. And before you ask me, darling, I don't mind the drudgery and the tedious jobs and the ugliness of it a bit. After all, I'm lucky I can train right here and can come home every night. I might get ahead faster at some big city hospital, but Dr. Litton is grand to me, and the nurses treat me like an adopted child, and where else could I find a better spot? For my first year or two, anyway."

"So long as you are happy and satisfied, child," said Elizabeth contentedly.

Later, at the table, Martha told the aunts about Jordan Ainslee. The small village on whose outskirts the nursing home was located had been thrown into something of a twitter at the discovery that Jordan Ainslee, one of the ten most eligible young men in America, perhaps in the world, was a patient at the nursing home. And so far no one save the nurses and doctors had seen him. So Elizabeth and Arleen listened with keen interest as Martha gave a carefully expurgated version of her first meeting with Jordan. There was, of course, no mention of judo or of Beelzy's unpleasant remarks, though she finished laughingly, "And it wound up by his asking me to dinner."

Elizabeth and Arleen put down their forks and stared at her and then at each other, shocked.

"Of course I told him it wasn't permitted," Martha finished hastily, her heart sinking. For she should have known at the very beginning that Arleen and Elizabeth would raise heck at the bare idea of her dating such a man as Jordan Ainslee.

"Well, I should certainly hope so!" said Arleen swiftly. "The idea! A girl like you out with that—that awful young man!"

Martha hesitated and then she said awkwardly, "But Aunt Arleen, he—well, he seems *nice*."

"A man with his reputation? A man who is in a nervous-disorders hospital, having the liquor and—er—worldly dissipation boiied out of him? A man who is in one scrape after another about some—some creature of a woman? My dear child!" said Elizabeth sharply.

Martha nodded. "Oh, well, I told him that even if Dr. Litton permitted it, you wouldn't," she confessed.

Arleen and Elizabeth exchanged swift glances and it was Arleen who spoke.

"Darling, it isn't that Elizabeth and I want to keep you from your normal destiny of marriage and a home and all the rest of it," she said earnestly. "We'd be the happiest people in the world to see you married to some worthy young man. But it would break our hearts to see you become—well, involved with some dreadful person like Jordan Ainslee. You must understand that."

"Of course I do, but you don't need to worry," Martha assured them gaily. "Goodness, the man forgot what I looked like ten minutes after I left his room. He hasn't been allowed any visitors since he came; privately, I think, it's that horrible little creature, Beelzy, who gave the orders for him not to have visitors. But you should see the two women who have come up to see him. One of them blonde and as beautiful as Marlene Dietrich, and wrapped in mutation mink and dripping with orchids; the other a sultry brunette in tweeds and red fox who threatened to tear the building down, brick by brick, if they didn't let her see 'darling Jordy'."

"Heavens!" gasped Arleen and Elizabeth in chorus.

Martha laughed.

"Dr. Litton got rid of them; he's a genius at that!" She dismissed it lightly. "But if you could have seen them, you'd know just how unlikely it is that a man like Jordan Ainslee would take a second look at the likes o' me when he knows women like that!"

"Well, then he's a very foolish young man!" said Arleen sternly. "Because you're a very beautiful girl, my dear."

"Pretty is as pretty does." Elizabeth signaled Arleen with her eyebrows not to overpraise the child, and Martha watched them with loving amusement. They were such darlings, these two spinster sisters of her father's who had taken her, a scared orphan, in and had given her their love and their devotion. Not for anything in the world, she told herself warmly, would she ever do anything that would hurt or distress them!

Which was why, a week later, she looked across a dinner table at Jordan Ainslee with surprised disbelief in her eyes. She Still couldn't quite figure out how it had all happened. A week ago, nothing in the world had been farther from her intentions than to be dining out with Jordan Ainslee at a road house thirty-five miles south of the nursing home. The fact that she had lied to Arleen and Elizabeth about where she was going; that she had bought a new dress to wear; that she had worn her jade-green spring coat despite the chill of the March evening—all of this swept over her as she sat looking across the table at Jordan, who had just given the waiter their order.

"What's up? You look scared to death!" said Jordan, puzzled.

Martha clenched suddenly cold hands in her lap and nodded.

"I am, I think," she admitted frankly. "I'm wondering how this all happened. My being here like this, I mean. I didn't intend to have dinner with you, or lie to my aunts."

Jordan was puzzled. "Why should you have to lie to your aunts to come out with me? Don't they allow you to have dates?"

"Oh. of course they do, but—well, they don't know you." Her voice stumbled a little, and Jordan's jaw tightened.

"But they do know my reputation and they don't think much of it." he said dryly, and studied her with a look in his eyes that was so warm and caressing that it made her heart leap a little "Would it help any if I told you, Martie my love, that I'm a much maligned young man? That not more than half of the outrageous gossip about me has a shred of truth in it?"

"I'm afraid it wouldn't." Martha admitted frankly. "Because even if only half of it's true that would be more than enough for Aunt Arleen and Aunt Elizabeth."

"Frankly, baby, I'm afraid I'm not too interested in the aunts." admitted Jordan, a little annoyed. "It's you I'm interested in. What do *you* think about things? Not your aunts or the doctors at the hospital or the nurses you quote, but you yourself—what are *vou* like?"

She smiled at him.

"Like nobody who could possibly interest you one tiny bit, Mr. Ainslee—not a bit like that glamorous Miss Durant, nor the lovely Mrs. Tallent who came to see you the first week you were there."

"Very few people are, baby," Jordan assured her dryly, and there was a wry look in his eyes. "They are beautiful, I grant you, but they have cash registers where hearts are supposed to be. Let's not talk about them. Let's talk about you."

And to her own surprise, they did throughout the dinner, which was surprisingly good. The waiter was incredulous when it developed they were not drinking, and when Jordan grinned ruefully and said. "Doctor's orders," the waiter looked properly sympathetic and understanding.

"You see," Jordan told Martha when the waiter had gone, "I promised Dr. Litton if he'd let me out of the hospital for a dinner date tonight, I'd be a good little boy and drink nothing. And you see, I'm keeping my promise."

"Well, of course," said Martha cheerfully, as though it were unthinkable that he should do anything else. "Otherwise, you'd be cheating yourself. It doesn't hurt Dr. Litton if you drink; it only hurts you."

"Right," said Jordan curtly. "And now let's talk about other things."

It was an evening that Martha would never forget. What they ate she could never remember; how she felt as they danced she would never forget. Jordan held her closely, his cheek against her hair; the feel of his arms about her made her blood warm and begin to leap. Against him, Jordan could feel her young heart pounding unevenly, and he hid a small smile that was touched with cynicism. Take 'em as young as you could get 'em, he reminded himself dryly. He looked forward with ardor to the return to the hospital. He and Martha alone in the back seat of the car, Beelzy at the wheel. And he'd beat Beelzy's ears off if Beelzy offered the slightest protest or interruption.

Jordan was so sure that Martha would drop into his hands at the first sign of his interest, so certain of her surrender, that the moment they were in the car and the glass panel that separated them from Beelzy had been slipped into place, he turned violently to Martha and took her into his arms. He was startled, most unpleasantly, when she refused to be taken; when she pushed his hands away with a gesture that had in it nothing of coquetry, and withdrew to her own side of the seat.

"It's been a nice evening, Mr. Ainslee. Let's keep it that way, shall we?" she asked, sweetly reasonable.

"But I'm crazy about you, Martha—I'm crazy for you."

He reached for her again, and again she put his hands aside, this time with a little gesture that indicated force would be applied if necessary.

"There's not much room in the car, but then of course the nice part about judo is that there are holds that don't require a lot of room," she said, her tone polite, conversational. Jordan sat back and glared at her furiously.

"Why, you—" he began, and strangled. Then after a moment he went on, his tone puzzled and curious now. "Martie, are you trying to say you'd use judo on me if I tried to kiss you?"

She considered that for a moment, thoughtfully.

"We-e-ell, no, not just if you kissed me," she said reasonably. "After all, you've given me a lovely evening."

"Then why not give *me* one? Martie—Martie—" His voice was husky, his handsome face was pale as he bent toward her.

Martha said huskily, "Keep your distance, mister."

But the gaiety was distinctly wobbly, and Jordan noted it with secret delight. So she wasn't as cool, calm and collected as she wanted him to believe, eh? He smothered a chuckle deep in his throat, and his hands touched her lightly.

Once more she tried a gay approach to what was rapidly becoming a problem.

"I've always wondered why cats like to be stroked," she stammered faintly.

"So now you know," he said very softly as he drew her close and held her tightly.

Almost in the instant that he drew her to him, and his mouth sought and found her own, he knew that she was stingingly conscious of Beelzy at the wheel. He was shut away from them by the sliding glass panel, unable to hear, but she knew that his bitter, sardonic eyes were on the rear-vision mirror and that he was trying hard to probe the darkness of the back seat. And despite her smothering sense of delight in Jordan's caresses, the knowledge made her self-conscious and awkward. Until at last Jordan let her go almost roughly, thrusting her away from him, and she knew that he was sulky and angry.

"I've thought a lot of things about you, Martie, since the first time I saw you," he said harshly. "But I never thought you were cold, frigid."

"I'm not," she protested hotly, her own anger rushing to meet his that hurt her at the same time as it frightened her. "But I'm not a wanton either."

"Few of my girlfriends are," drawled Jordan unpleasantly. "You're not a wanton, but you're a damned little innocent. You never slept with a man, did you, Martie?"

She gasped as though the question were a handful of ice cubes flung into her face.

"Certainly not!" she flamed, furious that he could even ask such a thing, hot and embarrassed and on the verge of tears.

"A shame," said Jordan dryly. "You've missed a hell of lot of fun, Martie. So have some men you might have honored."

"I can't see it as fun."

"How could you, when you don't know what it's all about?" he pointed out reasonably, and then his tone became more cynical and she knew he was laughing at her. "Saving it for Mr. Right-and-Only, Martie?"

"And what's wrong with that?" Her voice shook a little.

"Oh, wrong—right—who the hell knows what's wrong or what's right?" He seemed to be enjoying this, and she set her teeth hard and clenched her hands tightly in her lap and wished she had never come out with him. "Ever read Professor Stace's *The Concept of Morals*, Martie?"

She felt a little dazed and bewildered, and without waiting for her to answer he quoted lazily, " 'Nothing can be morally wrong which does not cause, or tend to cause, injury (unhappiness or decrease of happiness) to a fellow being.' And what possible injury or lack of happiness could you cause me, Martie, by letting me show you what fun love-making can be?"

"I don't want to talk about it."

"Neithet do I," said Jordan with unexpected force, and she was once more in his arms, and he was holding her tightly. And this time when he kissed her, she gave a small, frightened whimper; for it was as though, beneath the power and the storm, beneath the almost violent urgency of his demand, her heart flowered and burst into a sky-rocket that went dancing off among its fellowstars that looked coldly down from the dark night sky.

Jordan held her tightly despite her small, instinctive gesture of rebellion; and his kiss warmed her mouth until it gave back the kiss, and she no longer fought him. Any will to resist went out of her, and she could only cling to him. whimpering like some small, frightened animal, surrendering her young body to the ardent demands of his; forgetting everything in the rapture and the incredible ecstasy of that moment, so blazingly unlike anything she had ever known before.

Up front, Beelzy swore luridly under his breath, took the fork of the road that led away from the hospital for a long, roundabout road back, and his eyes were bitter, his mouth a twisted, ugly line. But he knew the boss better than to dare anything more than to extend the drive, without offering any protest, even though he saw the boss stepping heavy-footed into the middle of another mess. These dames! These hungry-eyed little dames, always swooning around the boss, hot-eyed and clinging—but with their whole thought centered on the boss's dough. Cheerfully, Beelzy would have confined the last woman on earth to the pits of Hell, and felt the world much better off without her.

CHAPTER THREE
INNOCENT WANTON

THE PLUMP, MIDDLE-AGED Negro maid opened the door to Beelzy and looked at him with cold hostility.

"Whut you hangin' 'roun' hyeh fo'?" she demanded grimly.

"I want to see *your* boss about my boss. And shake it up, Mamie; I ain't got all day," Beelzy. snapped.

"Miss Lisbeth won't be up for a couple of hours."

"Tell her to get her gorgeous body out of the hay and give a listen, Mamie, or she'll be warming chairs in agents' offices before spring breaks," snarled Beelzy.

Mamie stared at him in alarm that melted the hostility.

"Something's happened to Mr. Ainslee?" she asked swiftly.

"Yeah—a cute little nurse that's taking him over the bumps, but good! Now do I see your boss?"

"Man, you sure do, and quick," said Mamie. She vanished into the bedroom, from which Beelzy heard an angry, querulous voice, followed by the soft murmur of Mamie's soothing tones. Then Lisbeth Harlow appeared in the bedroom doorway, and Beelzy had a grim wish that the boss could see her like this just once!

Lisbeth, her hair protected by a hair net, remnants of night cream still visible on her lovely face, looked every day of her almost thirty years.

"Well, Bad News, this is a surprise," she said sharply.

"Ain't it, though?" growled Beelzy. "I hate you less than I hate this little pill-pusher, though, so I come to tell you that if you want to keep your claws in the boss, you'd better get up to that damned booby-hatch and make it fast. On account of he's really going overboard this time."

Lisbeth selected a cigarette from a handsome crystal box on the table, lit it, drew smoke deep into her lungs and said curtly, "Spill it."

"What else am I here for?" snapped Beelzy. "She's a cute little trick about five feet two, eighteen or nineteen years old, never had a man before—"

"Before?" Lisbeth shot at him swiftly, and Beelzy's ugly mouth twisted into a little grin because he was enjoying this moment, for all his worry about the boss.

"Before last night in the back seat of the Cadillac," he told her flatly.

"Oh, not Jordy; he wouldn't be so crude."

"Well, have it your way." Beelzy turned toward the door. "I just thought I'd tip you off. The boss is nuts, and I don't know where it'll wind up; you're his kind—she ain't. But now I've told you what's goin' on … "

He turned toward the door, gave her a little gesture that was a flip of his calloused hand, and went out. Behind him, as he drew the door shut, he heard sounds of activity and grinned a little, satisfied. Lisbeth would take off for that nursing home like a bat out of hell, in all her warpaint and feathers, and the boss would see her beside the nurse, and that would be that.

Martha had debated with herself whether she would go to Dr. Litton and ask to be relieved of waiting on Jordan. But that would call for an explanation, and the only one she could offer was the truth and that didn't bear thinking about. And so at ten o'clock, as she had done each morning since Jordan had been a patient at the nursing home, she went down the corridor with her uncapped head high, unaccustomed color high in her cheeks, and her eyes ashamed and frightened.

"How could you, Martie?" she had moaned to herself this morning on waking up, forgetting the exquisite ecstasy that was like pain; forgetting everything except that ugly fact that last night she had been seduced, with her own consent (not to say active co-operation), at which thought she had cringed and buried her face in the pillow. How could she face Jordan this morning? Yet how could she escape it?

She set her teeth hard and dropped her hand to the doorknob and promised herself that she would simply hand the tray to Beelzy and get out without even seeing Jordan. There was very small comfort in that thought, for while one part of her mind wanted nothing but to run away and hide, the other part of her—the bad part, she told herself sternly—ached to run to Jordan and to fling herself into his arms and know once more the mad, exquisite delight of surrender.

She opened the door, drew a deep hard breath and lifted her head as she stepped into the room. But Beelzy wasn't there, and beyond the bedroom door stood open. There wasn't a sound, and she stood for a moment listening, and hope and disappointment both flowed into her. Hope that she could escape seeing Jordan, for he was probably out in the grounds exercising; disappointment that she would not see him after all. It was a complex emotion that left her shaken and bewildered, as she moved forward to put the tray on the table beside the bed.

Behind her a voice said warmly, "Good morning."

She gasped, whirled, and the tray slid out of her hands. Glass tinkled on the floor and there was a spreading stain as the eggnog spilled.

Jordan stood, laughing, just back of the door, his eyes warm and adoring as they took her in from head to foot.

Martha put up a shaking hand to her throat and looked down at the spilled liquid and stammered something idiotic; she could never afterward remember what.

"That's all it's good for—to wipe up the floor," said Jordan. He came swiftly and took her in his arms and held her closely, his cheek against her hair. He was in pajamas and a thin silk robe, and the warmth of his body reached her through the thin covering, and her blood pounded and her pulses raced.

"Hello, honey," said Jordan very softly, his mouth against her own. "I've been waiting hours for you to see if you were as sweet and lovely as when I saw you last You are—you're even better."

Sharp confusion overtook her and she struggled against him, her face scarlet, her eyes ashamed, unwilling to meet his own.

"Oh, please, we—you mustn't," she stammered as she felt him urging her gently, yet inexorably toward the freshly made bed. "Someone—Beelzy—will come."

"I sent Beelzy into New York this morning—on business!" said Jordan, and emphasized the last two words. "And there's a 'Don't Disturb!' sign on the outside door, and furthermore it's locked. And don't think you're going to get away from me, baby, because you're not. I've waited a long time for you—hours and hours."

"I'm not even sure I want to get away from you," Martha stammered wildly. She hid her face for shame against his shoulder, and clung to him, crying a little.

Oddly enough, her tears made Jordan more gentle with her. He held her less tightly and no longer urged her toward the bed. His cheek against her hair, he was saying lightly, tenderly, "Darling, silly darling! Don't cry! What's there to cry about? Don't you love me?"

"Oh, yes, I do, I do!"

"And I love you, so what's there to cry about?" he crooned softly.

She looked up at him, flushed, tearful yet laughing in spite of the tears, and her voice shook a little. "Nothing at all, darling. I'm just a silly chump. Didn't you know that all women weep when they are happy?"

"Do they, now?" said Jordan, marveling.

Suddenly, even as he drew her closer and bent to kiss her, the telephone rang shrilly, persistently. Jordan swore furiously, and all but thrust Martha away from him so he could scoop up the telephone and bark savagely into it, "Well, what do *you* want?"

A startled look touched his face at whatever the answer was, and for a moment he stood rigid, holding the telephone tightly, before he said grimly, "I gave no orders that I was not to have visitors. If it's all right with Dr. Litton, by all means have her come up."

He put down the telephone and stood for a long moment, his brows drawn together as he stared down at the instrument. And Martha stood stiffly there, sharply conscious of the ludicrous situation. One moment she had been about to be taken to bed by this handsome stranger; the next the telephone had broken the whole situation.

"Saved by the bell," she stammered idiotically, trying desperately to remove the drama of the situation, to turn it into the farce it should be. "I'll mop up this mess."

Jordan only stared at her, still frowning, the look in his eyes remote, as though he hadn't the faintest idea who she was or how she came to be there. He moved past her into the living room of the suite and she heard the soft "snick" as the key was turned in the lock.

Hot-cheeked, half sick with shame, she worked automatically until the floor had been neatly wiped, the broken glass put on the tray. Then she hurried out of the bedroom and across the living room, not even looking at Jordan who stood at the window, his back to the room, his hands jammed deep in his pockets.

Before Martha reached the outer door it swung open, and the woman who stood there surveyed the room for a moment, her head up, her shoulders back. She was every inch the trained actress making a dramatic entrance, pausing long enough for her audience to take in every detail of the absurd bat cocked aslant on her sleek black head, the bluegray tweeds, the sable scarf twisted about her wrist like a bracelet.

"Jordy, darling!" she cooed sweetly, her sea-green eyes flicking Martha and dismissing her disdainfully.

Jordan turned, facing the room, his hands still jammed in his pockets, his face dark and set.

"Hello, Lisbeth," he grated. "You always choose the damnedest times for your entrances."

"Sweetie-pie!" protested Lisbeth, hurt, wide-eyed, gaily sweet. "They told me you'd had a physical, not a nervous breakdown! Is *that* all the welcome you have for me after I've pulled myself out of bed at the crack of dawn and driven almost a hundred miles to get here?"

"Barely sixty miles, my sweet," drawled Jordan grimly. "And I doubt if you've been to bed at all."

"Oh, but I have. Why, darling, I'm keeping positively barnyard hours since you've been ill! To bed with the chickens and up bright-eyed at the crack of dawn," protested the lovely intruder. Then she glanced at Martha again, and said insolently. "I suppose you're the maid Run along now; Jordy and I want to be alone."

Martha's eyes flashed.

"I'm not the maid," she said icily. "I'm Mr. Ainslee's nurse."

"Are you, now?" Lisbeth gave her more attention, and her lovely eyes narrowed just a little as they took in Martha's fresh, dainty youth and loveliness. "D'you know, Jordy darling, I don't seem to care for this set-up a bit? I don't think I'm going to like your little nurse—get rid of her immediately."

Jordan said harshly, "Stay where you are, Martie."

Martha flung him a swift, grateful glance.

"But I have my work," she began, and edged toward the door.

"Martha, this is Miss Harlow, who has appeared in a few of my plays," said Jordan harshly. "Lisbeth, this is Miss Desmond, who has been taking excellent care of me since I've been here."

Lisbeth looked Martha over with a look that made Martha feel as though those angry, hostile green eyes were peeling away her garments one by one and leaving her naked and shivering.

"I don't doubt it, I don't doubt it. Excellent care, I haven't a doubt," said Lisbeth, and her very tone deepened the insult. "Well, you can run along now, my dear; I'll take care of Jordan in the future as well as I have in the past, you may be sure. *If* you know what I mean—and I feel sure you do."

Martha met her eyes squarely, and though her face was brick red with shame and humiliation, Martha spoke softly and clearly. "I'm quite sure I do, Miss Harlow."

"So now you can run along and offer yourself to some other good-looking patient. I'm sure a place like this fairly crawls with them," said Lisbeth shortly.

"It will be a pleasure." Martha's voice stuck in her throat and the tears were there, too; tears of shame and humiliation and of a loss almost too bitter to be borne, as she moved toward the door.

Lisbeth, ignoring her as though she had already left the room, looked at Jordan, amused, self-confident in her knowledge of her own loveliness and her ability to handle him.

"Darling, I'm a little disappointed in you," she cooed sweetly. "Can it be your good taste has begun to slip badly? It's high time you were coming home, darling, before you do something foolish!"

Jordan studied her for a long moment, his eyes cool, touched with hostility. And as Martha's hand touched the doorknob, and he saw her shrinking aversion to the ugliness of the scene, Jordan took a swift step forward, caught her. and with one arm about her, turned to face Lisbeth.

"We hadn't expected to announce it quite so soon, Lisbeth, but you may as well be the first to know," he said quietly, evenly. "Martha and I are going to be married."

Lisbeth caught her breath and her eyes widened. But even as she glared she saw the white, stunned look on Martha's face, and the look of incredulity in the wide brown-gold eyes that Martha lifted to Jordan's face. And Lisbeth laughed, though it was a laugh entirely free of amusement.

"Darling Jordy, you are so funny—like a bad little boy who won't grow up," she teased him with an arrogant assurance that tautened the line about his jaw. "Do you expect me to believe such nonsense? The girl gave it away the moment you spoke. It's obvious that you are just trying to tease me, but it's not nice of you to use her that way."

Martha was staring up at Jordan, scarcely hearing Lisbeth's confident taunt. Jordan, looking down into Martha's young, innocently ardent eyes, softened a little and grinned and bent his head and kissed her. Lisbeth's hands tightened inside her smart gloves.

"Marry me, Martha?" asked Jordan softly.

For a breathless moment a radiance that was almost blinding blazed in Martha's eyes, and then the light went out and she tried to draw herself away from him, white-faced and hurt.

"Don't—don't try any harder to make a fool of me, Mr. Ainslee," she pleaded huskily. "You've succeeded far better than you could have hoped."

"Let the child alone, Jordy," said Lisbeth sweetly, but there was venom in the green eyes. "Shame on you. Why, she's only a raw little kid."

"I mean it, Martie," said Jordan softly, ignoring Lisbeth. "You said just now you loved me, and *I* said I loved you. I'd have asked you to marry me then if we hadn't been invaded."

Lisbeth caught her breath at the word and stared from one to the other, dazed and incredulous.

"Please, Martie?" said Jordan very softly. He kissed her tenderly, yet with undisguised, unashamed passion, before whose warmth Martha's uneasiness, her doubt, her discomfort melted. "I'll be very good to you, Martie."

"This nonsense has gone far enough, Jordy," cried Lisbeth hotly. "You're making a fool of yourself—and of her—and of me. You're mine, Jordy, and you're not going to marry anybody!"

Jordan flung her a cold, hostile glance.

"Want to bet?" he asked.

For a moment they stared at each other, and all that they had ever been to each other was forgotten as a gulf widened between them. For a moment there was a flicker of panic in Lisbeth's eyes.

"Jordy, you're out of your mind," she panted.

"Martie?" said Jordan very softly, and kissed her again.

"Oh, yes, Jordan, yes! I'd love to!" said Martha softly, unsteadily. She cradled herself in his arms, forgetting in the wild, exciting rush of her blood the white-faced woman who stood staring with completely dumbfounded eyes.

After a moment, Lisbeth said huskily, "I give in, Jordy. I don't know what it is that you want of me, but whatever it is it's yours. Now get rid of her. Send her away. She's served her purpose—I'm licked."

Jordan looked at her and laughed and tightened his arm about Martha, who was glowing like a rose. She was feeling the hard, uneven thudding of his heart against her close-pressed cheek, loving the sheer masculine scent of him. *His wife!* The breathless excitement of that thought shook her to the very depths of her being and but for his arm about her, she could scarcely have stood erect.

"I want nothing from you, Lisbeth—haven't I made that plain?" said Jordan so softly that for a moment the menace of his words did not quite register with Martha. "And you can expect nothing from me, ever, unless it's a part in a show I'm casting—a part that suits you and that you're capable of playing. So now, why don't you run along? Can't you see that Martie and I want to be alone?"

Lisbeth, clinging to the back of a chair for support, her face quite white beneath the deft make-up, her eyes more gray than green now, said huskily, pleading with him, "I know why you're doing this to me, Jordy. It's because of Whit. Of what I was to him. I told you I'd never seen him since you became my lover."

"And spent the weekend with him the first week I was here in the hospital. Don't lie, Lisbeth; you do it so badly." Jordan's tone was acid with bitter amusement.

Lisbeth winced, but went doggedly on.

"You can't mean to mess your life up like this, Jordy. Not to tie up with some silly little innocent." Her voice broke.

Jordan looked down at Martha and his arm tightened about her.

"She's innocent, Lisbeth, but she's got the makin's of a mighty sweet little wanton, too. An innocent wanton—what man could ever hope for more?" said Jordan. He laughed a little as Martha blushed and hid her face against him.

"You can't do this to me, Jordy." Lisbeth's words were a whimper of pain.

"Why can't I? I never made you any promises, beyond providing you with the luxuries to which you hoped to become accustomed, and those promises have been kept in full measure, as I think even you will admit," Jordan told Lisbeth grimly. "You can keep the apartment; the rent is paid for the year. And you can keep the presents I've bestowed, and they have been expensive ones, remember? You chose them yourself. But you have no strings on me at all, Lisbeth—that's the way it's been from the first."

"But I can't stand by and see you wreck your life."

"Please, Lisbeth, let's not have any third-act curtains," said Jordan dryly. "You're not a good enough actress to put 'em over. Let's make it a good, clean break."

Lisbeth drew a hard breath and flung up her head.

"I'll believe that you're going to marry her when I see you do it," she said through her teeth.

Jordan laughed.

"That's an idea," he said lightly. "Hang around and be our witness. You and Beelzy ought to be able to see a good job well done. By the way, where *is* Beelzy?"

A rather subdued voice outside the partly opened door said, "I'm here, boss."

Beelzy came and stood before Jordan, but would not meet' his eyes. Jordan's eyes went from Beelzy's downcast face to Lisbeth's white, ravaged one, and his eyes brightened a little.

"Oh, now I get it! You sold me out. Beelzy, you went to Lisbeth and brought her here."

"I drove myself," Lisbeth cut in sharply.

"In the convertible that was your Christmas present from me? I hope it was a nice drive," said Jordan with icy amusement. And to Beelzy he said savagely, "You're fired, Beelzy."

"Sure, boss," said Beelzy heavily and without surprise. "When do you want the car?"

"Now, as soon as I get some clothes on. You and Lisbeth are going to a wedding, Beelzy—won't that be fun?" said Jordan, and laughed.

Beelzy looked up sharply and Martha shrank a little from the fury and the hate in his eyes. But Beelzy only said quietly to Jordan, "Sure, boss, if you say so."

CHAPTER FOUR

PRODUCTION
PREPARATION

"SCARED?" JORDAN LAUGHED softly as he drew Martha into his arms and settled her on the deep back seat of the car.

Martha was staring with wide eyes at the narrow gold band that encircled her third finger, and her color was high.

"Scared?" she repeated. "I'm your wife, Mr. Ains—"

Jordan gave a little shout of happy laughter, and up front, at the wheel, Beelzy ground his broken teeth with rage.

"Darling, now that you're my wife, don't you suppose you could call me 'Jordan' right out loud in public?"

The breathless excitement of the crowded day rushed over her like a movie montage. There had been quite a scene with Dr. Litton when she and Jordan had stood before him announcing their marriage She didn't like to remember Dr. Litton's hurt, indignant eyes, for it hadn't been a nice trick she had played on him, rewarding his kindness and his goodness by eloping in this outrageous way with his most famous patient; and Jordan's bland refusal to stay at the hospital for any further treatment had added to Dr. Litton's resentment.

"It's your own life, Martha," he had said grimly. "I only hope you know what you're doing. And as for you, Mr. Ainslee, you haven't been exactly the most co-operative of patients. You are by no means well, and you should stay here at least another month. However, if you don't wish to ... "

Jordan had laughed and drawn Martha close to him and asked lightly, "Another month in a hospital, Doctor, when I have a beautiful and alluring new wife? What kind of honeymoon would that be? And besides, Martie's going to be good for me— and good *to* me—aren't you, darling?"

Martha went scarlet even now, hours later, remembering Dr. Litton's cold disapproval. The scene with the aunts had been even worse; they had been so hurt, so bewildered. They hadn't liked Jordan—but then, she rushed hastily to defend him even in her thoughts; they didn't really know him as she did. They'd love him as she did, once they were exposed to his charm and his good looks and his appeal.

And then there had been Lisbeth's ravaged face, her incredulous eyes as she had listened to the frowsy old justice of the peace pronounce the ceremony that had made Jordan Martha's husband. It was as though Lisbeth had not been able to believe that Jordan really meant to go through with it until the last words had been said, and Jordan had kissed Martha with frank passion. Then Lisbeth had drawn a deep hard breath, and her eyes had met Jordan's for a long moment.

"Aren't you going to congratulate me, Lisbeth? I'm a very fortunate man, indeed," Jordan had said lightly.

"I'm going to wish Martha luck and a lot of it, for she's going to need it," Lisbeth had flung at him through her teeth. She had immediately stumbled into her convertible and sent it flying recklessly back toward New York.

"Hi," said Jordan softly, and Martha brought herself back from her confused memories of the crowded day to realize that she was here with Jordan, in his handsome, expensive car, and that they were rushing toward New York and a life as Mrs. Jordan Ainslee that was so new to her it practically scared her to death.

"Remember me? Ainslee's the name—and what might *your* name be, my pretty?"

He was in such high spirits that suddenly to Martha he seemed almost frighteningly young and boyish, but she strove valiantly to push aside all the chaotic thoughts and to concentrate on meeting his mood.

"Im happy to know you, Mr. Ainslee. My name is Mrs. Jordan Ainslee," she said gaily. But it was a slightly unsteady gaiety, and suddenly it broke and she added, her voice awed, "Why, I *am* Mrs. Jordan Ainslee. I can't believe it!"

"You better had," said Jordan, and his tone was low now, throbbing with a note that set her heart racing like mad and that jerked her pulses into a mad leaping that was unlike anything she had ever known before.

After a moment, his arm still holding her close, he chuckled.

"Will you ever forget Lisbeth's face when the old dodo said 'I now pronounce you man and wife?' It was a sight to see," said Jordan with such happy relish that for a moment Martha shivered.

"She—she's very much in love with you, Jordan," she said uneasily, her voice stumbling just a little over the name. "I felt sorry for her."

"You're wasting sympathy then, angel," Jordan told her dryly. "Lisbeth loves nobody but Lisbeth, and the thing that brings that lovely glow to her eyes is a bankbook with nice round numbers in it.

For a moment Martha sat silent, loving the warmth of his arm about her, and then she said reluctantly, "There was another woman who came to see you—a lovely blonde."

She felt quickened interest in his touch, even before she heard it in his voice.

"Faye was there? Faye Clarke?"

"I think that was her name."

"But I don't remember seeing her," Jordan's brows were drawn together in a puzzled frown.

"She wasn't allowed to see you."

"Allowed? What the hell are you talking about? I wasn't a prisoner. I went to that dump of my own free will and it was merely for a rest—why wasn't I allowed visitors? Here I've been thinking none of my so-called friends cared enough—"

"There was a notation on your card at the reception desk that you were not to have visitors," Martha told him. "I have no idea whose order that was."

Jordan stared straight ahead at Beelzy, who was giving all his attention to his driving, and suddenly Jordan raised his voice as he leaned forward, speaking very distinctly.

"Would you know why I wasn't allowed to see Miss Clarke, Beelzy?" he asked.

"Some of them saw-bones thought you wasn't strong enough," Beelzy began hurriedly.

"Oh, no, they didn't, Beelzy; you're the guy who gave that order. Don't lie about it," said Jordan sharply.

Beelzy's thick shoulders moved in a little gesture that might almost have been called a shrug and he said over his shoulder, "So, okay. It was dames and twists like the Clarke and the Harlow that put you up there. I felt like you needed a rest from 'em."

"I ought to twist your thick neck," said Jordan through his teeth.

"Any time you'd like to try it, boss," said Beelzy grimly.

Jordan sat back and looked down at Martha, almost as though the moment she had been out of his arms he had forgotten her. For a moment he stared down at her as though wondering who she was or how she got there. And then suddenly he grinned and once more his arm was about her, holding her close.

"Well, hello there!" he said happily. "Fancy meeting you here."

Martha relaxed against him, but that small, faint edge of uneasiness that had attacked her at his reaction to her first mention of the lovely blonde did not vanish. This man she had married, this man who had possessed her physically, just as now she knew he would possess her in all the other ways a wife belongs to her husband, was a stranger. An almost frightening stranger. But even as the thought crossed her mind, Jordan's caressing hands touched her intimately, deftly, and her whole being seemed to melt beneath his ardor. ...

From the very first night in Jordan's apartment, a night of ecstatic fulfillment and exquisite delight. Martha felt like an intruder The apartment was a large, luxuriously furnished one. There were two servants, a middle-aged couple—who looked upon Martha with cold, measuring unfriendly eyes and made her feel like a not-very-bright ten-year-old There was Beelzy, cold and unfriendly, as definitely hostile as he dared to be. And there were Jordan's friends and acquaintances, the fawning sort that swarms about a man who is rich and has power in their field. With Jordan this was, of course, the theater, and so his friends and acquain-tances were, in Martha's private estimation, a motley crew. Lisbeth was well in the forefront of the welcomehome parties.

People looked curiously at Martha, who felt queer and uncomfortable in her smartly sophisticated, expensive new clothes which Jordan had ordered for her from a celebrated shop. She stood for weary hours while being fitted with all sorts of cos-tumes, hats, shoes. Even hats, she found to her dazed surprise, in this strange new world in which she found herself, were designed and made to order and had to be fitted—sometimes half a dozen times before the very eccentric young man who was. at the moment, "the last word" in hats, was satisfied.

There were parties, parties and more parties. Jordan was popular—any man with his wealth and power would have been, of course, but he was popular for himself, as well. He had some friends that Martha knew instinctively were fond of him because he was Jordan Ainslee, not because he was insanely rich and powerful in the theater world.

After the first wild orgy of shopping, when she was quite sure her wardrobe contained more clothes than half a dozen girls could ever wear, Martha found herself with idle hands. Nothing to do from the time she and Jordan breakfasted around noon until the night's activities began. Jordan was reading plays, making plans for fall production, and Martha was worried about him. He was too thin, he was nervous, strained; but when she tried to protest at his working schedule and remind him that he had been ill, he turned on her in surprising anger.

"For heaven's sake, Martie, forget that you were once a pill-pusher. I'm all right. I don't need a nurse. I don't want a doctor. I just want to be let alone—is that clear?" his tone one of biting anger.

Martha drew back as though the blow had been physical, and her eyes blazed.

"More than clear," she told him hotly. "For all I care you can fling yourself out of the window."

She caught her breath and her eyes flew wide and her face went white.

"I didn't mean that, darling—oh, I didn't mean that!" she wailed like a terrified child.

Jordan, jarred out of his irritable mood, laughed a little and caught her in his arms and held her closely.

"Of course you didn't, dearest, and neither did I," he comforted her. "I'm a cross-grained old fool, honey lamb, and you're an angel to put up with me. Let's cut the shenanigans tonight, and have dinner at home and go to bed early. Shall we?"

Radiant, starry-eyed, Martha breathed, "Oh, yes, darling!"

Jordan looked down at her for a moment and there was the tiniest possible shadow in his eyes, but Martha was too radiantly happy to be conscious of the shadow. Nor was she sufficiently sophisticated, perhaps, to understand it if she had seen it.

Early in July he found a play he liked and plunged headlong into the work of preparing it for production. He was away from home for longer and longer periods as time passed and actual rehearsals began. Lisbeth Harlow had a part in the new play and purred with the satisfaction of a cat when she boasted to Martha about it.

CHAPTER FIVE
MARTHA ON THE LAW

THERE WAS A hectic time while the show finished its rehearsals and then went out of town for its tryout. Martha had confidently expected to go with Jordan, but at the last moment he had said coaxingly, "Look, honey lamb, why don't you run up to visit your aunts for the two weeks I'll be out of town? A tryout is a wild and hectic business. We'll be rewriting and polishing and I'll be at the theater twenty-four hours a day, practically, and all the people you know who are connected with the show will be working like slaves, and you'll be bored to death. Run home and see the aunts and prove to 'em I haven't beaten or starved or mistreated you, and then when I get back and the show's settled down, you and I will go somewhere for a trip."

Martha was pleased with the plan, and the aunts were enchanted to see her. It was fun showing them her lovely clothes and Jordan's gifts of expensive jewelry and the car he had bought for her and which she had learned to drive for herself. But she was lonely for him, and the time seemed to pass with leaden feet until she could return to New York and await Jordan's arrival.

The tryout had proven the show was good; there was every hope that it would have a long run. Martha prepared to help Jordan celebrate by planning a special dinner the night of his return. He would be tired, and they would have dinner at home, and he would tell her all about the show—and they would be together again. He had missed her and yearned for her, she told herself, radiant and flushed at the thought.

It was Sunday and the train would be in at four-ten. By four-thirty she began expecting him, running to the window, laughing at herself for such folly, for it was sixteen floors to the ground and she could not have seen the car drive up, anyway.

But as the time passed and it became five o'clock and then, years and years later, it was six, and then it was seven, there was still no sign of him nor any word from him.

It was midnight before she heard his key in the lock, and roused a little from her deep chair beside the window where she had dozed a little out of sheer exhaustion.

Jordan came in, and before she could pull herself to her feet, she saw that he was not alone. Lisbeth Harlow, exquisitely groomed and beautiful as always, came in beside Jordan and stood laughing, arrogantly sure of herself.

Martha's heart had done a somersault at her first sight of Jordan and the blood had leaped in her body. But at sight of Lisbeth, she sat very still for a long moment, her lower lip clenched between her teeth,

"Hello, Martie," said Jordan, and made no move to come to her, to scoop her into his arms, to cradle her close as she had ached and hungered to be held.

"Hello," said Martha huskily, and waited, because there had entered the room with these two *a* bitter ominous warning, a knowledge that something unpleasant was going to happen.

"Remember me, Martie?" purred Lisbeth, her voice slurring and insolent. "Sorry we were late. But we stopped off at my place for—cocktails, shall we say?"

Jordan said quickly, "Martie, there's something I have to say. and it isn't easy."

"Why not, darling?" Lisbeth cut in. "I don't find it hard at al). I've known it all along and I think Martie has begun to suspect.

It's just that he's discovered his marriage to you was a mistake, Martie, and he wants you to be a nice girl and give him a divorce."

Jordan said savagely, "I can tell her myself."

"Then why didn't you, darling?" asked Lisbeth, sweetly reasonable. "There's no point in trying to do it bit by bit."

"No," said Martha huskily, above the roaring in her heart, the rending, tearing noise in her ears as her whole world fell into dusty bits about her. "No, there's no point at all." She set her teeth hard to keep back the tears.

She was so stunned, so dazed by the terrific suddenness, the complete unexpectedness, that she felt powerless to move. She could only huddle in her deep chair and stare with dazed eyes at Jordan.

"I'm sorry as hell, Martie; it's a dirty trick," Jordan began.

"It isn't at all, darling," Lisbeth cut in, once more with that air of sweet reasonableness. "After all, no one can expect you to stay married to a little simpleton."

"Lisbeth!"

For just a moment Lisbeth looked faintly frightened, and then she smiled up at him and tucked her hand through his arm and pressed her ripe body against him.

"I only meant, dearest, that Martha's inadequacy as a lover —" she began.

Martha gasped and pride pulled her to her feet. She looked at Jordan out of eyes that were dazed and uncomprehending.

"You—you told her *that*, Jordan?" she whispered unsteadily, as though she could not believe her ears.

"Of course not," Jordan began swiftly.

"He didn't have to, Martie," said Lisbeth softly. "Don't you suppose I know Jordy well enough to know things like that? When he came back to me, I knew you had failed to satisfy him, that the marriage was a mistake, just as I told him it was in the very beginning. And of course, Martie, if you hadn't been so innocent, you'd have known that the only reason he rushed you into marriage was to spite me! We had quarreled and he was jealous and he hit back at me by rushing you off your feet—and it wasn't a nice trick, Jordy; it wasn't nice at all!" She turned to scold him fondly with an air that said she would not find it difficult to forgive him.

"Don't be such a bitch, Lisbeth," said Jordan savagely, and took a step forward toward Martha, who shrank from him and lifted eyes that were dazed and bewildered with pain. "Martie, dear, try to understand," he began.

"I do understand; I understand thoroughly," stammered Martha above the pain that was tearing at her heart. "You want to be free to marry her, and you shall be. Just as quickly as I can get a divorce."

"The Virgin Islands, Martie—you'd like that—it would suit you," drawled Lisbeth, her eyes dancing just a little as though she were thoroughly enjoying the suffering of this girl who had dared to take Jordan from her, even if only temporarily.

"I'll find a place," said Martha thinly.

"I'll make a settlement on you, Martie—you shall never want for anything," said Jordan, his voice soft with remorse.

"I don't want anything you've got to offer, ever!" Martha flung at him. "I want only the clothes I came here with; I have a little money."

Jordan, annoyed, feeling like a heel and resenting the feeling, turned his resentment on her.

"Oh, now, there's no sense in behaving like a child!" he protested.

"Why not? I *am* a child. You've both made it very plain. And I don't want your money and I wouldn't accept it if I were starving!" Martha countered furiously. "I've got enough to pay for a divorce and I can always get a job."

Lisbeth cut in as Jordan would have protested, "Oh, let the child alone, Jordy. Don't fight her. If she wants to preserve her few small scraps of pride by turning down the settlement, let her do it. After all, you owe it to her to let her decide that much."

"Thank you," said Martha through her teeth, her young eyes bitter. "I hope you two will be very happy, and now get the hell out of my way!"

The unexpected oath was so startling to Jordan that he gave way before her as she ran up the stairs and banged shut the door of the bedroom.

For a moment Jordan stood staring at the steps, and Lisbeth watched him anxiously, yet with a trace of sardonic amusement in her eyes.

"Never mind, darling, she'll get over it," she soothed him tenderly after a moment. "She's young and she'll outgrow it. But you and I, Jordy—we're going to be the happiest two people that ever lived."

"I suppose so—with the thought of what we've done to Martie always beside us. That ought to be one hell of a lot of fun!" said Jordan through his teeth.

Lisbeth inserted her body into his arms and caressed him with the small, deft, expert caresses. When at last they turned to go back to her apartment, the image of Martha and her white stricken face, her wide, sick eyes had begun to fade a little before Jordan's eyes. ...

Martha had no thought of sleep. She felt she could never again lie in the bed she had shared so gloriously with Jordan; she winced as at a cruel blow when she thought of Lisbeth's lovely, musical voice saying sweetly, "Martha's inadequacy as a lover—" She had been uneasy, unsure of herself, and Jordan hadn't done anything to help her. She put the knuckles of one clenched fist hard against her teeth and fought with every ounce of courage and strength she possessed to keep back the tears.

She found the suitcase in which she had brought her own belongings to the apartment and began to pack swiftly the modest wardrobe that had been hers when she came. But as she folded and tucked things into the suitcase, a thought stopped her: where would she go? Not back to her aunts, to see pity for her and fury for Jordan in their eyes. No, she couldn't go there. And Reno was out of the question. She didn't have money enough to go to Reno; her bankbook showed a little over three hundred dollars of her own money. The handsome allowance Jordan had given her was not to be touched, of that she was determined. And she would not take with her so much as a scarf for which he had paid. Lisbeth had spoken of "her small scraps of pride." Well, they were small and tattered, but they were all she had left and she would not sacrifice them.

She sought back in her mind as the hours passed, and eventually she remembered a woman who had been a patient at the hospital. She had just returned from getting a divorce and she had a "crack-up" afterward that had necessitated a stay at the hospital. Martha, in her first probationary months, had spent a good deal of time with the woman—what was her name? Brand? Brand?—who had taken a fancy to her. The woman had gotten a Florida divorce; she had spoken of a little fishing village on the west coast where expenses had been small.

It was almost dawn before Martha had managed to dredge up from the back of her memory the name of the little fishing village, and had made up her mind that she would go there. If she was very careful, the money she had might stretch for the required length of residence necessary to permit the divorce; and when she was divorced, she might go on maybe to Miami, or Palm Beach, or one of the large towns and continue her training as a nurse. She had attained some small degree of calm by the time she had reached her decision and had begun to formulate her plans. But though her conscious mind was very busy with plans, her subconscious was still tortured and crying out endlessly against the pain of losing Jordan; of being "inadequate." She knew it to be the sharpest, most devastating insult one woman can offer another.

She had just finished dressing in the dark blue suit with the matching hat and shoes that had been her wedding costume, when there was a knock at the door and she opened it, standing back, startled, because Beelzy stood there.

Before she could speak, Beelzy nodded as his eyes took in her traveling costume, the locked bag at her feet.

"That's kinda what I thought you'd do," he commented. "Take it on the lam."

"What do you want?" demanded Martha sharply.

Beelzy spread his thick, calloused hands.

"Nothin'—except to tell you that I'm on your side."

"That's a surprise, and you won't mind if I don't believe you, will you?"

Beelzy's ugly face was touched fleetingly by a brief grin.

"Hell, no, I didn't expect you to," he admitted. "But just the same, I think the boss has gone off his nut and ought to be locked up somewhere—away from all dames—for failin' again for that Harlow twist."

"I don't wish to discuss it."

"You're gonna walk out and let her have him, without even liftin' your dukes?" asked Beelzy, stating a fact rather than asking a question.

"Just what did you expect me to do?"

"Just what you are doin', o' course," sighed Beelzy. "Damned shame, though. I think you and the boss could a made a go of it if the Harlow dame hadn't come in. 'Course, you could stay and fight."

"For something I no longer want?" said Martha curtly, and turned away so he would not see the look in her eyes.

"Yeah, I guess you're right," agreed Beelzy after a moment. "No 'dame could ever forgive a guy for sleepin' out while he was still on his honeymoon. I'll have 'em send your car around."

"You can call a taxi for me, if you will. The car is no longer mine," said Martha slowly and distinctly.

Beelzy stared at her, caught by something in her tone.

"Oh, now, wait a minute," he protested.

"What for?" The sleepless night, the ache in her heart, the accumulated longing for Jordan through the long, long weeks that had just passed—could it be possible it had been only two weeks?—had worn her nerves raw, and her voice shook. "I don't want to talk about it, Beelzy. I just want to get out—fast!"

"You mean you ain't goin' to nick the boss?"

"I mean I don't ever want to see him, hear of him, or be reminded of him as long as I live," said Martha through her teeth, and caught up her suitcase and moved toward the door.

CHAPTER SIX

FIGHT WITH AN OCTUPNS

MARTHA STOOD IN front of the sun-blistered little cafe that was the Pine Hill bus station and looked about her with dazed eyes. She thought that she had never seen a more desolate spot, beaten with the clublike rays of the mid-day September sun. Mrs. Brand—or was it Bland?—had been here in the winter time, and she had spoken fondly of its quaint aspect, its quiet and peace. In the glaring blaze of the blinding sun, Martha could see nothing quaint, though it was certainly quiet!

Across the road, paved with millions of white shells long crushed into coarse gravel, there was a small, tired-looking building across whose one window the words, "Groceries; Fishing Tackle; Bait and Boats" had faded until they were barely legible. At the back of the building a ramshackle pier led out to where there was a small landing float, and against it were tied several boats. Along the road where she stood there were a few houses, all with peeling paint, all half smothered in the swiftly growing, almost rank tropical shrubbery of hibiscus, oleanders and masses of yellow allamanda. Nothing human stirred.

She had been the only passenger leaving the bus here and the driver, sun-tanned, casual, had grinned at her and said mockingly, "You'll be sorry, lady! Sure you've got the address right? This is Pine Hill, you know."

"Yes, I know," said Martha, and managed a smile. "No, I haven't made a mistake, but thank you."

The cafe proprietor had awakened enough to stare at her as though the sight of a passenger alighting from the noonday bus were such an unheard of thing that it couldn't possibly be real.

"Hotel?" he repeated her question, when the bus had vanished in a cloud of white dust. "Why, lady, there ain't no hotel here. Nor a boarding-house, neither. Folks that come to Pine Hill come mostly for the fishing and there ain't no fishing this time o' year. But when the folks come mostly they rent a cottage from Lafe Hendrix that runs the grocery and handles the renting of boats and things."

"I'd rather have a cottage, if it isn't too expensive," said Martha eagerly.

The cafe proprietor grinned.

"Well, Lafe'll stick you if you let him," he said confidentially. "Winter times, he gets ten dollars a week for a small cottage, twenty for one that'll take care o' a crowd. But this time o' year — how long would you be stayin', lady?"

"Three months," said Martha, and saw the man's eyes narrow a little and color poured into his face.

"Takin' the cure, eh? Well, we don't get many o' them," he admitted frankly. "Mostly, folks down here gettin' a divorce want a place that's a little more lively than Pine Hill. Still and all, if you go over and tell Lafe you want a cottage and you won't pay him no more than twenty-five dollars a month, and you won't be here but three months, chances are he'll let you have it."

Martha had thanked him warmly, and the middle-aged, slightly grubby-looking little man waved a dismissing hand, and as she started for the door, added, "If you git tired fixin' your own meals we serve a right tasty meal—sometimes."

Martha laughed, thanked him, picked up her suitcase and crossed the white road, blinking at the glaring sun.

The store was dark and cool, faintly musty, smelling of kerosene oil, mosquito spray and coffee. Martha stood for a moment adjusting her eyes to the dimness. When she could see more clearly, she discovered the enormous old man who sat sprawled in an old Morris chair beside a window open to whatever breeze the blue Gulf beyond might offer. The man's head was bald, save for a fringe of silky-looking white hair across the back of his head. His enormous round face with its triple chins had been sunburned to an almost leathery color. He wore a shirt that was open to the waist, the sleeves cut out, and his faded blue denim pants had been cut off well above his enormous sun-bronzed knees.

Martha stood still for a moment, staring at him, wide-eyed. Suddenly the old man spoke, without even opening his eyes.

"Better git out o' that sunlight, lady. It's powerful bright down here—kind o' like a X-ray. Not that *I* mind, o' course, but wimmen are funny critters."

The old man chuckled and opened his eyes that were twinkling a little as he looked up at Martha.

"Mighty fine, mighty fine," he rumbled, and Martha raised her head haughtily. "What can I do fer you, ma'am?"

"The cafe proprietor—" Martha began.

"Biggest crook 'tween here and Tampa," snorted the old man. "And that's takin' in a heap o' territory, ma'am. Don't believe for sure no more'n half o' what Bill Edwards tell you. What *did* he tell you, by the way?"

"That you had some cottages to rent," stammered Martha. The old man looked surprised.

"Now, whut's got into Bill, him tellin' the truth for once in his life?" he wondered mildly.

"Do you have a cottage?" began Martha, who was hot and tired and in no mood for such nonsense.

"Sure I got a cottage," said the old man. "Got five or six of 'em—take your pick. Any one you want fer—" his eyes traveled over her shrewdly and he finished—"fifty bucks a month, lights and water included."

Martha said quickly, "I couldn't pay that much."

"Down here for a divorce, ain't you?" snapped the old man so unexpectedly that Martha caught her breath and took a backward step. "Dunno why a gal that looks like you would want to hole up at Pine Hill fer a divorce, but there's them as do. Ain't no other reason, as I know of, why a gal that looks like you would come to a place like this. And if you can't pay fifty bucks a month rent, then I don't need to ask how come you're here instead of a more lively place. Takes money fer them places. How about twenty-five a month?"

Martha smiled in grateful relief.

"Oh, that would be wonderful," she glowed.

"Ain't nothin' wonderful about it, but you're welcome to it." The old man heaved himself, groaning, out of his chair, straightened his massive body, scratched his belly and yawned. "Well, come on, let's git started. Reckon you want to git unpacked."

He lifted her suitcase and strode ahead of her out of the store and along the blinding white road, leaving Martha to trot along behind him as best she could.

The road wound between tall sand dunes and curved a little, and there before her was a row of bleached little cottages, perched on stilt-like foundations, at the very edge of a wide, pale-yellow beach against which the turquoise waters of the Gulf splashed and broke in lazy white breakers. There was a breeze here, and Martha sniffed the salt of it delightedly as the old man strode up the step's of one of the little cottages and crossed the porch that shook ominously beneath his weight

He thrust open a door and peered inside, and sniffed in disgust. Martha followed as he went from one room to another, thrusting windows open and batting aimlessly at the fine dust that lay over everything.

Martha quailed as she looked about her. Three rooms, that was all. A fair-sized living room with ancient wicker furniture, its cushions long ago ruined by age and salt water and dampness; a kitchen with an antique oil-stove perched on four bricks, its container empty, its burners rusty and stained. A bedroom with a rickety-looking iron bed. a thin but lumpy mattress and *a* cotton spread that was faded until its original color had long been forgotten. A few rickety chairs scattered about, a battered old wooden ice-chest in the kitchen; a strip or two of worn matting scattered indiscriminately about.

The old man studied her and grinned wryly.

"Ain't exactly the Biltmore," he admitted. "Still, you ain't exactly payin' Biltmore prices, come to think of it."

"No, of course not," Martha admitted honestly, and managed a smile. "It's fine. I'll be very comfortable here."

"And that's as big a lie as Bill Edwards ever told," the old man said dispassionately. "Still and all, it's the best Pine Hill's got to offer and it's about the cheapest thing you're gonna find anywhere in the state."

He put down her suitcase in the bedroom and came back.

"Send you up some kerosene and some groceries," he flung over his shoulder as he stalked out. "Reckon you ain't fool enough to try to eat at Bill's place; you don't look like you was rugged enough to be able to take that kind o' grub."

Martha followed him to the porch, fumbling in her bag.

"I haven't paid you yet." She fished out a slim roll of bills, and the old man's hand curled covetously about the two tens and a five she gave him, even as his eyes traveled up the beach to where a lone figure was striding along, bending now and then to pick up and examine a shell. "That's your nearest neighbor—crazy as a loon, but folks feel like he's harmless. Just don't have nothin' to do with him; he belongs up at the other end o' the beach, anyway."

As if there were no more to be said, he stalked down the steps and back along the path, while Martha stood still, staring after him, wide-eyed and shaken.

Maybe she had been a fool to come to this little isolated place just because a patient she had once tended had spoken of its "quaint charm, its utter quiet and peace."

She swept and dusted, and when she found half a bar of strong laundry soap in the kitchen, she scrubbed as best she could. And when at last the place looked a little less bleak and distinctly more clean, she was so hot and tired that the turquoise waters of the Gulf were an irresistible lure.

As she put on her bathing suit, her thoughts touched the daring Bikini suit that Jordan had bought for her but she donned a plain two-piece swim suit that was meant for swimming and not for parading the beach. With her hair tucked beneath a white cap, she ran down the steps and across the beach and plunged into the cool, stimulating water.

She splashed and dived and swam until she was cool and a little tired, and then waded toward the beach. A floating something like an old blue sweater danced toward her on the waves, and she struck at it idly with her hand—and the next instant, knew horror so sharp that it all but stunned her. For the floating blue thing at which she had struck so casually came to horrible life, and the ragged-looking tentacles wound about her fingers in a grip that burned as though she had thrust her hand into live coals.

For a moment she was too stunned, too shocked to do anything but stand still, staring at the horrid pinkish-blue worm-like tentacles wrapped tightly about her fingers and at the bluish mass that still floated, and terror and pain sent her staggering toward the beach, screaming wildly. The water tried to hold her back; she shook her hand furiously and some of the tentacles broke off and the big blue mass floated away. But her hand was on fire and the pain was almost unbearable.

From somewhere she heard a man's voice crying sharply, "Stand still—don't touch it with your other hand!"

And then someone's arm was about her wet, shaking body and a hand protected by a bath towel was removing the worm-like things from her fingers, and then she fainted. ...

When she regained consciousness she was on a leather couch in a musty old room, and a stout, elderly man with a grizzled mustache beneath the kindest, most patient eyes she had ever seen was bending above her, watching her closely.

For a moment she remembered nothing; and then the agony in her hand brought back memory and she started up, screaming.

"Now, now, now," soothed the tired-eyed old man, pushing her back on the couch. "Just lie still and let the morphia take effect. It's going to hurt for quite a while, but I've given you as much morphia as I dare. Just try to endure it as best you can—it'll wear off."

"What—what was it?" Martha stammered, wincing with the pain, panting a little.

"Paul here says you slapped at a jellyfish—one of the breed called a 'portugee man-o-war'—and it slapped back at you," said the man, smiling a little. "I'm Dr. Barton. Mighty glad I was here in my office instead of out on my rounds when it happened."

A man who had been hovering in the background, anxiously watching her, came forward, smiling tentatively.

"And I'm mighty glad I happened to be on the beach when it happened," he said quietly. "Hendrix should have warned you about swimming there, this time of the day. The jellyfish have been unusually bad this year—I'd have stopped you if I had seen you in time."

Martha had her teeth set hard in her lower lip, and tears were slipping down her face, though she was trying desperately not to cry.

"I—I never heard of things like that," she stammered faintly.

Somewhere a telephone shrilled violently, and the doctor picked it up, spoke briefly and urgently, and then turned back to them.

"An urgent call," he said crisply. "Baby on the way, and I've got to beat the stork if I can. Paul, I'll take the lady to her cottage on my way."

"Sure, Doc," said Paul, and scooped Martha up in his arms, and carried her down to the street where an ancient jeep stood in the broiling late afternoon sun.

He sat down in the jeep, Martha in his arms, and the doctor slid under the wheel. The drive to the cottage was a matter of minutes, and as Paul got out, still carrying Martha, the doctor flung up a hand and went racing back down the road.

Martha, out of the mists of pain and shock that still gripped her, said shyly, "Please put me down—I can walk."

"Nothing of the kind," said Paul firmly, and strode up the steps, kicked the door open, and deposited her gently on the lumpy bed. He eyed the massive bandages about her wounded hand and arm. "You've got to get out of that wet bathing suit and into something cool. Where are your clothes?"

He rummaged in the drawer of the old bureau, brought out a thin cotton nightgown, eyed it, nodded and came back to Martha. When he bent to put his hand on her, Martha gasped and drew away from him.

"Please!" she protested, shocked, outraged. "You've been very kind, but I can manage now."

"Don't be an idiot—with all the bandages on that hand?" snorted the man.

"No, please!" she stammered wildly.

The man straightened and glared at her, his hands on his hips. He was tall and rangy, and his body was burned brown, and he wore nothing but swimming trunks. His hair was thick and sun-bleached and he was not at all good-looking. And now he was angry.

"You silly little fool!" he raged furiously. "If I had wanted to attack you, I certainly wouldn't have taken you to a doctor and then brought you here. I have a better sense of timing than that."

"I'm grateful, truly," stammered Martha miserably. "But I can manage. Honestly I can."

From outside came a hail, and Paul glared at Martha furiously before he stalked out. Martha managed to get out of her suit and into the cotton gown and beneath the thin sheet, while her ears strained to hear mingled voices outside, and decided that Lafe Hendrix had kept his promise to send up supplies, and was undoubtedly being regaled by the news of her adventure.

She listened, and then gradually she relaxed. The pain in her hand and arm was growing easier, and her eyelids were growing heavy. Almost without being aware of it, Martha slipped into a slumber so deep that it was like a black pit of oblivion in which not even the pain could make itself felt.

CHAPTER SEVEN
RETURN TO NURSING

SHE AWOKE IN the morning with all the symptoms of an unpleasant hangover. Her head felt enormous and as though stuffed with cotton; there was the traditional dark brown taste in her mouth and a very faint feeling of nausea when she lifted her head. With her first conscious thought, she realized the "hangover" feeling was due to the morphia. She looked fearfully at her bandaged hand and arm—and sat bolt upright, nausea or no nausea. For her hand and arm were no longer bandaged, and there was not the slightest mark to remind her of yesterday's terrifying and agonizing experience.

She stared at her hand, turning it this way and that, and touched it with the fingers of her other hand. It seemed incredible that so painful an experience should not have left the slightest mark! She had felt sure that she would be horribly scarred by the burns.

A voice spoke from the open door, a voice that was ever so faintly touched with teasing laughter.

"Can you imagine?" said Paul, looking freshly scrubbed in tan slacks and a sport shirt. "All that pain and not a single mark less than twelve hours later."

Martha laughed a little.

"I almost resent it," she admitted frankly. "To suffer like that and have no scars to show—" She rummaged in the thin bedclothes, which consisted chiefly of a coarse, many-times washed cotton sheet.

Paul, lounging in the doorway, chuckled.

"If you're looking for the bandage, thinking it might have slipped off in the night, Doc Barton would resent that bitterly; his bandages don't slip, as he himself would be the first to assure you." he told her lazily, a twinkle in his dark eyes.

Martha looked up at him, puzzled.

"Then what happened to it?" she demanded.

"I took it off a couple of hours ago, because I was afraid it would be hot and make you uncomfortable," he told her cheerfully.

Martha stared at him, wide-eyed, pulling the sheet up instinctively to her very chin, and above it her eyes were enormous in her suddenly pale face.

"You—why—you—" she stammered faintly.

"I've been here all night, and your reputation is practically in shreds and tatters," he told her cheerfully, his eyes laughing a little though his mouth was unsmiling. "You're an abandoned woman, and you may as well face it."

"That—that would be about all I needed—" she stammered, on the verge of tears.

"To be sure of a divorce?"

She caught her breath and her eyes blazed.

"How—how did you know?" she stammered.

"A goldfish bowl gives a tremendous amount of privacy compared to what you find in a dump like Pine Hill." he told her dryly. "Of course, the entire populace—three hundred and ten, counting the forty-two-odd, some of them extremely odd dogs—knows all about your set-to with the man-o'-war yesterday. It was considered nothing but downright neighborly of me that I 'sat up with the sick' last night. And you were plenty sick in the night. Natural result of what had to be almost an overdose of morphia to deaden the pain—and I hope it's all gone this morning?"

Martha lifted her hand, flexed the fingers and stared at it

"I'm not sure now which hand it was," she marveled.

"Good!" said Paul. "Well, how about some breakfast?"

"Coffee, perhaps."

"Coffee coming up," said Paul briskly. "Can you manage or do you need a maid?"

His eyes laughed at her, but Martha flushed.

"Ob. no, thank you, I can manage beautifully," she assured him.

For just a moment longer Paul stared at her, a little puzzled.

"If you'll forgive me saying so, you're less like a gal seeking a divorce than any woman I ever saw. Sure it wasn't just a lover's spat and you rushed off before you had time to think?" His unexpected frankness made her gasp.

She elevated her pretty chin a little and met his eyes.

"I'm quite sure," she told him evenly. "My husband left me for another woman."

"Then he's a damned fool and deserves whatever happens to him, and I hope it's plenty," said Paul grimly, and stalked out of the room.

Martha lay still for a moment, staring at the closed door. And then suddenly, frightened lest he return, she slid out of bed and hurried into a thin cotton dress left over from last summer in the country. Its color was a cool blue and her flame-colored hair was held back from her face by a matching blue ribbon that made her look like a child.

When she came out into the living room, Paul had spread a gaily patterned paper cloth on the table, and was setting out the cracked and chipped crockery that he had found in the makeshift cupboard in the kitchen.

"You'll soon learn to follow my example," he assured her cheerfully. "Disposable dishes, to be tossed into the fire when you've finished with 'em, thus removing one of the greatest bugaboos of housekeeping, which is known as dishwashing!"

"Oh, but I like to wash dishes," protested Martha.

Paul stopped and stared at her as though he had never seen any one like her before in all his life.

"I don't believe it!" he said flatly.

Martha laughed a little, finding that she liked him.

"But it's true," she assured him. "I'm a very domestic creature."

And suddenly, painfully, she was remembering Jordan's annoyance when, on the servants' night out, she had invaded the kitchen and prepared a very good dinner indeed, so that she and Jordan might be alone. But Jordan had had other ideas, and the excellent dinner had gone into the garbage can and she and Jordan had gone out to a dinner party.

"And that was something Friend Husband didn't like?" said Paul quietly, and she looked up, almost startled to see him there.

Her young face was touched with bitterness and there was a mist of tears in her eyes that she could not quite blink away.

"One of the many," she said dryly.

Paul nodded, his mouth tightening.

"Somehow I'm beginning to feel I could dislike that guy one hell of a lot without half trying," he said grimly. And before she could answer he had gone back to the kitchen to get the coffee.

When he came back he seemed to have forgotten what they had been talking about, and was very gay and blithe throughout the meal, so that Martha, interested in what he was saying, ate almost without realizing it.

When they had finished, he said briskly, "Now I've got to get to work."

He grinned at her, unashamed, as he indicated the dishes.

"And since you simply adore doing dishes, I wouldn't be selfish enough to deprive you of the pleasure," he assured her handsomely.

Martha laughed as she rose from the table and faced him. "You've been terribly good to me," she began impulsively.

Paul looked down at her gravely, and unexpectedly his hand cupped her pretty chin and tilted her face upward, and he said softly, "And I have a hunch I'm going to be terribly good for you!"

And to her stunned surprise he bent his head and kissed her lightly, and while she was still speechless, he walked out of the cottage and a moment later she saw him striding along the beach with long strides toward his own cottage at the far end of the beach.

She had cleaned the little cottage and had brought an old beat-up canvas deck chair out to the shady corner of the rickety porch when she heard the sound of a jeep, and saw Dr. Barton waving at her as he got out of the little vehicle and came up the steps.

"Feeling fit this morning?" he asked cheerfully, smiling at her. "But still a little groggy from the morphia, of course. That will pass. You'll be chipper as a redbird before you know it."

"You've been very kind, Dr. Barton," said Martha gratefully. "I'll get my purse—I want to pay you."

Dr. Barton stared at her, puzzled.

"For what?" he demanded.

It was her turn to stare, caught by surprise.

"Why, for taking care of me."

"My dear girl, no doctor worth his salt in a place like this charges for such an emergency," Dr. Barton assured her firmly. "After all, it's the town's responsibility—we are supposed to warn people when there are jellyfish about, and if we don't, we are legally responsible for damages. Would you settle just for my services?"

Martha laughed a little at his pseudo-worried tone.

"Well, of course!" she assured him.

"You won't sue?"

"Well, for goodness' sake, who would I sue—the Gulf of Mexico or the jellyfish?" she laughed.

"There are those who would sue the city—imagine calling Pine Hill a city! And anyway, the town's broke, so a suit would do you no good at all." said Dr. Barton cheerfully. "Did Paul take good care of you last night? He promised me he would."

For no good reason at all, Martha's color rose, which the doctor's wise old eyes did not fail to note. And her voice was a little hurried when she answered.

"I'm sure he did," she said quickly. "I sort of passed out pretty soon after we got here and the next thing I knew it was morning, and be was here. He's nice, doctor. He said he had to go to work—"

"Work?" Dr. Barton snorted derisively. "That guy wouldn't know a job of work if it rose up and kicked him in the teeth. Know what he does? He collects shells!"

There was vast amused, if somewhat friendly contempt in the doctor's voice.

Martha's eyes were wide.

"Oh, *no!*"

"Oh, *yes!* Isn't it absurd? I thought it was only kids who wandered the beach and picked up shells," said the doctor. "It seems, from what Paul tells me. quite a thing nowadays—societies of shell collectors all over the country; they have a trade paper and all sorts of nonsense. According to him. there is money to be made in the 'shell game'."

Martha said, amused, "Well, at least it soulds like an easy way to make a living."

"If you're satisfied with being a beachcomber. Judging from Paul's way of living, I wouldn't say there was a great deal of money in it," commented the doctor, and then he chuckled richly. "Come to think of it, though, I don't recall ever hearing of any Wealthy country docs, did you?"

Dr. Barton leaned back in his chair, smiling to himself and enjoying a moment of leisure. Then he sat forward looking straight at Martha.

"Word around here is that you were a student nurse before you were married," he said. "How would you like to help me out—I can promise I'll keep you from getting bored. Life in these parts may be dull for most people, but the country doctor has more than he can do."

Martha was immediately elated at the idea. Working with Dr. Barton would certainly be valuable experience and she was anxious to go on with her career. Also it would keep her mind off Jordan.

"Oh, Dr. Barton, that would be wonderful. It will be good to get back to work again."

Dr. Barton heaved himself to his feet, smiled down at her and, bidding her good-by, said, "See you, then, tomorrow at eight-thirty when I start on my rounds."

Martha sat watching as the little jeep bounced and shook itself out of sight around the sanddune toward the little town.

She had made up her mind since she had left Jordan that she was not going to look back. And now there was no need to look back—tomorrow morning she would be starting out again on the work she loved.

CHAPTER EIGHT

LESSON FROM A BEACHCOMBER

I N THE NEXT few days she and paul became good friends. During the days she was kept busy with Dr. Barton, then at nights she and Paul would have dinner together and afterward settle down for long talks or take walks along the beach. She liked him; he was gay, amusing. He was unexpectedly gentle and tender at times, and once or twice she saw a light in his eyes that made her just a little uneasy. But before she could be quite sure the light had ever been there, it was gone, and she could relax once more and bask in the knowledge that he was her friend.

He had begun to teach her something about shells, and as the subject began to open up before her, she found it increasingly fascinating. And then Paul took her on an expedition to one of the neighboring cays, far enough out so that the trip took over an hour by motorboat.

It was a beautiful morning, on the water there was an unexpected breeze, and the Gulf was dancing with tiny whitecaps. In the boat there was a picnic basket, and a giant thermos of water and a smaller one of iced tea. And Martha, in the briefest of blue linen shorts and a matching halter looked ten years old and as bright-eyed and eager as though she were no older. But her body, as Paul noted with a slight tightening of his jaw and a faint bitterness in his eyes, was anything but childish.

Martha's delight in the morning was as gay and young as her looks, and when they had landed on the shelving beach of the long, narrow cay with its few palms and its harsh palmetto growth, she began immediately on her search for shells. She brought her finds to Paul as eagerly as a child, and couldn't hide her disappointment when he had to tell her that though what she found was lovely it was neither rare nor valuable.

"I'm keeping them anyway," she told him when finally they sat down for lunch and a rest beneath the scant shade of a palm that leaned at such a precarious angle it seemed certain that the next gust of wind would destroy it.

"Keep them by all means, as a memento of an experience I hope you will never have again," said Paul grimly as he swung open the picnic hamper, and spread the gay crepe-paper cloth and wedged it down with heavy pieces of *coquina*. "Keep them so you'll never forget a beachcomber named Paul—or am I too ambitious?"

She took a hungry, enormous bite of the sandwich he offered her, and laughed.

"I'll never forget you," she told him gaily, "but 'ambitious' is hardly the word I'd apply to you."

Leaning back on one elbow, Paul inspected his sandwich gravely before he bit into it, and then he shot her a glance that she was too relaxed and happy to notice.

"You think I'm a complete bum, don't you, Martha?" he accused her.

"Well, I wouldn't exactly call you a go-getter who's likely to set the world on fire," she told him lightly, bending toward the picnic hamper for an olive.

"The world seems to be blazing right merrily without any help from me, don't you think? Whold want to add to such a conflagration?" he answered. But obviously his mind was not on what he was saying, and suddenly, caught by his tone, Martha glanced up and met his eyes.

For a long moment he let her look deep into his eyes. For a long moment he was unable to keep from his eyes his hunger for her. Martha had seen that look before and recognized it with a small shock.

Paul watched the color flood her face, saw her downcast eyes, the little instinctive gesture with which she tugged at the brief halter, and his hand clenched a little in the sand.

"Sorry," he said curtly. "But after all, you're a woman, Martha and I'm a man, and—well, you're damned attractive and I'm human. So what are we going to do about it?"

Martha was still now, her appetite gone, the sandwich lying half eaten on the sand, her hands tight together.

"We aren't going to do anything about it," she stammered at last through her teeth.

"Aren't we?" An odd look flickered for a moment in Paul's eyes and his jaw hardened a little. "I think we are, Martha; I think we have to."

"I'm never going to love anybody else," she told him, her voice high, shaking a little, tinged almost with hysteria. "It hurts too much."

"You sound even younger than you look when you say things like that, Martie," he said coldly, and saw her cringe a little at the name, and added, "I suppose that was *his* name for you—Martie?"

"It was everybody's name for me; it's always been since my father started calling me that when I was a baby. I was a very small baby and Dad used to say that 'Martha' was too heavy a name to hang on anything so small."

"You are still in love with Jordan, aren't you, Martie?" demanded Paul.

Martha caught her breath and her eyes flew wide.

"How did you know his name?" she demanded.

Paul stared at her in mocking amusement that was not entirely convincing because of the pain in his eyes.

"My dear child," he drawled, "did you really think that Pine Hill was so isolated that the citizens, to a child, don't know you are down here to divorce Jordan Ainslee, the millionaire playboy? And that everybody, once more to a man, woman and child, is calling him everything that means 'tight-wad' and 'heel' that he'd send you to a place like this, instead of to one of the plush caravansaries on the Gold Coast?"

"Coming here was my own idea," Martha told him, her chin held high. "It's all I can afford, and I wouldn't accept a cent from Jordan if I were starving."

Paul sat up and stared at her, frowning a little.

"Oh, come now, that's very silly," he began.

"I have to protect what tiny scraps of pride I have left," she told him harshly. "They—Lisbeth and Jordan—didn't leave me much!"

Paul was still studying her, his knees drawn up, encircled by his arms, the Gulf breeze blowing his thick dark hair.

"So in order to protect what few bits of pride you have left, you just walked out, handed your husband over to this Lisbeth creature, and did everything you possibly could to make things easier for them. Which, of course, will make them despise you."

"Jordan despised me before I left, and Lisbeth hated me from the moment Jordan married me," Martha cut in, and her young face was so white and ravaged that Paul ached with pity for her. Yet he went remorselessly on.

"Jordan despised you? That I find hard to believe. What possible reason—" he began. Martha's head was up and her eyes met his steadily.

"Because I was inadequate as a lover," she said thinly, and in her own ears it was not her voice, but Lisbeth's, rich, warm laughing, that said the words she had tried so hard not to hear, but that she could not escape hearing over and over again.

Paul stared at her, his brows drawn together in a frown.

GAIL JORDAN

"My good, sweet, lovely child," he exploded in a tone of complete incredulity, "you are out of your mind. No man alive could find such fault with you."

"Jordan could," said Martha thinly. "I suppose he was right. No man would tell another woman a thing like that about his own wife, would he, if it were not true?"

Paul was white with anger, his jaw ridged and set.

"No man would tell another woman a thing like that about his wife unless he were a fool and a heel!" he said through his teeth.

Martha said huskily, finding an odd sort of comfort in emptying her overfull heart to this man who was so suddenly, so completely her friend, "Well, I was a virgin, and Jordan had known so many women—he—rhe's not very patient or very gentle—" She broke off, and her face was scarlet with remembered shame, and for a moment she was quite still. Paul watched her, his mouth a set thin line, his eyes dark.

She looked up at him at last and smiled faintly, but it was a smile that had in it nothing even remotely resembling mirth.

"I guess the trouble is I—well, I think sex has been highly overrated as entertainment. I don't seem to care much about it." She broke off and turned her head away so he could not see her hot, flushed face.

"You poor little dope!" he said very softly, and, startled at his tone quite as much as the depth of his pity, she turned swiftly and stared at him, and Paul grinned a little at her expression.

"So you just walked out and let the other gal have him," he said at last. "You didn't stay long enough to fire a single gun in her direction."

"I didn't think it was worth it."

"You didn't care enough about him to fight for him?"

"How could I? I don't know how!"

"You're younger than she is."

She looked startled.

"Well, yes, but how did you know?"

"Because her way of working indicates an older woman. One of the things she resented most about you was your youth," said Paul simply. "It's always that way with that kind of woman. And if you wanted this guy back, it would be so simple—like taking candy from a baby—though I've seen some babies that would put up a terrific howl, at least, if you threatened their lollipops."

Martha said hotly, "You think I should have pleaded with him, begged him not to throw me out?"

"Hell, no! But I don't think you should have rushed out the moment you found the other dame was moving in," said Paul sharply. "You should have stayed and fought, with her own weapons."

"Which I didn't have, remember?"

He made a little gesture of dismissal with an angry hand.

"Your inability to satisfy the guy? Hell, child, that's only a matter of a little training and common sense."

"Neither of which I had, remember?"

His eyes took her in from the top of her flame-colored hair to the tips of lovely sun-tanned legs.

"Either of which you could easily gain, if you cared enough."

For a moment she digested that, and then the color flowed into her face and her eyes would not meet his. But Paul went on studying her, and now a new look had replaced the avid hunger that had, for a moment, frightened her. It was a measuring look; a look that took stock of her from head to foot. At last he nodded as though he had reached the decision he had expected to reach.

"Do you want him back, Martie?" he asked softly.

Martha caught her breath and for a moment she was with Jordan again, and his arms were about her and her whole being was melted into white hot fire. She drew a deep breath.

"Of course," she said unsteadily.

"Then you shall have him back," Paul promised her as though she were a child and he offered her something as easy to buy as a stick of candy. "Only you'll have to do exactly as I say, and trust me. Will you do that, Martie?"

Puzzled, Martha studied him for a long moment and his eyes met hers straightly, and after a moment he chuckled dryly.

"Sure, I'm crazy about you, Martie, and I'd give anything to have you," he told her grimly. "But I'm a funny sort of duck. I don't want a woman unless she wants me. If she's crazy about another guy, that lets me out."

Paul smoked, as unconcerned outwardly as though theirs had been the most casual of conversations, not at all as though he had spoken of things she felt should never, never be discussed between a man and a woman unless they were married. And yet there was a little uneasy gnawing at her mind. Was she too prim? A prude? Was that one of the things Jordan hadn't liked about her?

"Hello." Paul's voice, slightly dry, penetrated her thoughts, and she gave a little start and turned to him. "Remember me? I'm still here, you know."

"I was thinking," she stammered.

"So I gathered." His voice was still dry. "Only I would have said from your face that you were remembering. And not too pleasant remembering, either."

"No." admitted Martha huskily. "It wasn't."

Paul was silent for a moment, and then he looked down at her.

"Well? Have you made up your mind?" he asked.

"About what?"

"About whether you'd like to have Jordan back and thumb your nose at Lisbeth."

"I'd love it!"

"Having him back—or thumbing your nose at Lisbeth?"

"Both, I suppose."

Paul nodded.

"Then we'll get busy," he said firmly, and leaned toward her. "Come here, Martie."

That look was back in his eyes again, and it made Martha shrink from him, her own eyes wide and a little fearful. Suddenly Paul grinned wryly.

"On second thought, I guess we'd better go a little more slowly," he said dryly. "There are other important things to be attended to first. You must write Jordan that you have changed your mind and you want a settlement and it must be a hefty one. Or else you'll withdraw your suit."

"I don't want his money."

"Shut up," ordered Paul grimly. "You'll do as you're told, because the only way to get him back is to make him respect you. And the only way to make a man like Jordan respect you is to hit him where it hurts—in his pocketbook. Jordan likes expensive women."

"How do you know?"

"Because I know men like Jordan Ainslee. Why else did you think I was a beachcomber gathering shells for a living? Because men like Ainslee turn my stomach and you'd be surprised how hard it is to get where you never see one of 'em."

"Did somebody like Jordan injure you, Paul?" she stammered at last, because somehow she had a deep urgency to know.

Paul stared out over the dark waters of the Gulf and she saw the mirthless curve of his mouth.

"Just once," he said thinly. "And we won't discuss it, if you don't mind. I'm going to sleep."

And with no more than that casual, makeshift apology he lay back on the sand and went to sleep.

Martha sat crosslegged, staring at him, a little shaken, oddly disturbed. He wasn't good-looking, not in the spectacular manner of Jordan, anyway. He was tall and lean and he had what Martha described to herself as a "sort of craggy face." He was strong-looking, rugged even; his unexpectedly boyish grin took years from his apparent age. But when he was grave and stern-looking, she thought he must be old—probably thirty-five or even more.

She was studying him absorbedly when suddenly he sat bolt upright and she realized that he hadn't been asleep at all.

"Well?" he asked softly, and his eyes were gleaming, though he was smiling a little. "What's the verdict, Martie?"

"Oh, but I thought you were asleep," she stammered.

"Then you're younger and more innocent than I thought, Martie." His voice seemed warm as it reached out to her. "Martie, you don't honestly believe that any man alive and under eighty could possibly sit within five feet of you, in that—that postage stamp you're wearing—and sleep?"

She caught her breath and drew back a little, panic in her eyes, one hand flung up in a little instinctive gesture of protest.

"Relax," said Paul savagely. "I'm not going to fling myself on you like a ravening animal. I told you I liked a bit of active co-operation, didn't I? Only don't be such a damned innocent—asleep, indeed!"

Martha squirmed a little, and Paul grinned wryly.

"Stop looking at me like that!" she blazed at him furiously.

"Then stop looking like that!"

"I can't help the way I look."

"Why should you want to? You look fine, just fine!"

She was scarlet with confusion and discomfiture.

Suddenly Paul chuckled and turned his disturbing eyes away from her.

"Poor little Martie! It's not easy, is it—a virgin's mind and a harlot's body?" he said dryly.

She caught her breath as though at an insult.

'I'm not a prude!" she lashed at him furiously.

"Who said you were? And how would I know?"

And suddenly, illogically, to her undying shame, she burst into tears. Tears of exasperation and uneasiness she could not explain, but that shook her from head to foot with a stormy, violent sobbing.

Paul swore savagely, and stared at her in shocked alarm.

"Oh, now, for Pete's sake, cut that out!" he roared at her sharply.

"You make me so damned mad!" she sobbed, and fumbled for a handkerchief. Paul obligingly flung her a handful of paper napkins. "Thanks," she stammered as she scrubbed her face, her voice small and shaken. "I don't know what made me be such a fool. I'm not a crying woman—honestly I'm not. That's the first time—almost—that I've cried since—" She set her teeth in her lower lip to control its trembling.

"Since you left your husband?" Paul finished for her.

Her face twisted a little and her smile was thin-lipped and bitter.

"Since he left me," she corrected him.

Paul nodded, and watched her for a moment until she managed a faint, moist smile and held out her hand for the lighted cigarette he extended.

"I'm all right now," she said huskily. "Where were we?"

Paul studied her for a moment, and then he got to his feet and reached down a hand to draw her up beside him.

"Why, we were just starting out for a walk, weren't we?" he drawled. He did not miss the very slight touch of disappointment in her eyes and grinned to himself.

CHAPTER NINE
NIGHT OF ECSTASY

S HE WAS SO absorbed in her work with the people who lived in and around Old Pine that she lost track of time. And Paul was a most obliging and amusing acquaintance—she shied away from a warmer word—and she was getting interested in the "shell game," as Paul called it. They cruised the cays farther and farther. They returned from such forays with Martha always childishly excited about her finds.

The time she had found a "lion's paw," perfect and exquisite, they came back to her cottage and sat on the porch to watch the great golden moon lay a tremulous path of silver-gilt radiance across the tumbled silk of the Gulf. It was then that Paul spoke again of her regaining Jordan.

They had sat in silence for a long moment, relaxed, watching the fragile beauty of the night, when Paul suddenly leaned forward and tapped out his pipe against the porch railing.

"Still think it would be nice to have Jordan back?" he asked her so unexpectedly that she gasped and turned a startled, bemused face to his.

"Of course," she answered so automatically that Paul shot her a swift, suspicious glance.

"Sure it isn't just that you'd like to give Lisbeth a kick in the teeth?" he suggested dryly.

Even in the yellow moonlight she flushed, but her eyes met his steadily.

"That's part of it," she admitted frankly. "I—well, I know it's not noble of me, but I'd like to make her eat her words."

Paul chuckled dryly.

"It can be done, baby, it can be done," he drawled, and stood up. "Well, I'll paddle along now. You get to bed and get a lot of shut-eye. Tomorrow's a big day. The bus for Miami leaves the Sarasota station at eight-forty. That means we have to leave here on the six-ten bus."

She stood up, her face vivid with excitement.

"But why are we going to Miami?"

"As if you didn't know! First because they have a very fine beauty shop there that would be delighted to give you the works and make you look as sophisticated as you are lovely," said Paul, and his tone was derisive. "Also, they have some very excellent shops, which Pine Hill hasn't—or had you noticed that?"

Worried, Martha shook her head.

"But what about my work with Dr. Barton?"

"Martie, you've got to get this settled first, and then you can go on with this nursing of yours," Paul reasoned.

"I guess you're right, Paul. But I haven't any money, and I couldn't accept any from you."

"That's good," said Paul, "because I wasn't going to offer you any!"

She bit her lip in annoyance at her own stupidity. Of course he hadn't planned to offer her money, for he probably didn't have any too much of his own. But how else had he expected to finance tomorrow's expedition?

He answered her question before she could put it.

"You're going to check into one of the Beach's most expensive suites," he told her coolly. "Then you're going to put through a long distance call to Ainslee, and you're going to tell him you've changed your mind about a settlement; that you want five thousand dollars immediately, and that your attorney will discuss a settlement with his, or else."

"Or else?" she repeated a trifle dazedly.

"Or else you'll come straight back to New York, cancel out any divorce plans, and raise merry hell in general," Paul finished.

Martha considered the plan for a moment and then suddenly she grinned impishly.

"That certainly ought to rattle Lisbeth," she said happily.

"It'll probably set Ainslee's teeth on edge a little, but that will be an advantage. Anyway, why shouldn't he finance your campaign to seduce him again?" Paul's tone was unexpectedly bitter, and Martha stared at him where he stood above her, leaning against the porch pillar, his arms folded across his chest, looking down at her with an expression at which she could only guess, for his face was in the shadow.

After a moment she said huskily, "Maybe, after all, it would be better just to go on as I've planned. I'm not so very sure that I want Jordan back."

Paul went very still for a moment, but the darkness concealed his expression, and she could only guess at the effect her words had had by his voice when it came after a moment.

"Oh, come now, after all the many, many times you've told me how madly you're in love with him?" His tone was derisive.

"He's the only man I ever knew well," she confessed. "And I—well, I let him make love to me before we were married, and if I wasn't madly in love with him, what does that make me?"

"A wanton, I suppose." Paul's tone was more derisive than ever. "According to your lights, a wanton by all means; to my way of thinking, a pathetic little innocent."

Somehow, for some odd, crazy reason that she could not understand, that angered her. She stood up suddenly and in the yellow moonlight, her body gleamed like an ivory statue, faintly gilded, and with her head thrown back, she faced Paul almost fiercely.

"Pathetic, am I?" Somehow that had been the word that had flicked her on the raw. "An innocent, am I? Damn you, I'm a woman—a married woman—no, an ex-married woman. I'm about to be a divorcee. Don't you dare call me an innocent, or pathetic, either."

And before Paul could do more than straighten and stare at her, she moved swiftly, flung herself into his arms and pressed her warm, glowing body against him. For a moment he stood rigid, and then his arms went about her and gathered her hard against him, and his mouth sought and found her own.

For a moment he held her so; and then the almost prim kiss that she gave him, as untaught as a child's, laid a cooling hand on the fever that shook him, though it was one of the hardest acts of self-control of his whole life that he put her away from him, despite her clinging hands.

"You infant!" His voice grated against his clenched teeth.

"Don't go, Paul," she panted, and once more she was close and hard against him.

"Martie, have a heart," he pleaded. "You don't know what you're doing."

"I do, too," she panted. "I'm asking you—I'm begging you, Paul, to stay here tonight. To—to stay with me, Paul."

"Oh, Martie, for Pete's sake." His arms tried to push her away but she wasn't having any. She only pressed closer to him.

"Because how else will you know whether Jordan and Lisbeth were right?" she breathed, her mouth against his own.

"Because I've got sense enough to know they were wrong a mile—and I don't have to stay here to know that," said Paul grimly.

Martha said softly, "Don't you want to stay, Paul? Don't you want me?"

"Hell, yes," said Paul, his voice little more than an agonized sound. "But damn it, you're such a kid."

"I'm almost twenty," she told him hotly. "And I've been married and I'm going to be divorced."

"Hush that talk," he ordered her. But now his arms were tight and hard about her, and he was lifting her in his arms and turning toward the cottage door. "You—you tempting little devil!"

Martha laughed softly, contentedly, and her lips nuzzled his bare shoulder....

In the morning when she awoke it was very early. The sun had not yet risen, and outside there was a grayish, silvery light that told of the breaking of day. She yawned a little, stirred, and memory came back on a rising, flooding tide. Memory of such a night as she had never known or dreamed in all her life.

There was nothing of shame, nothing of regret in her emotion. Nothing but a startled, wondering delight that such happiness could exist. Almost fearfully she turned to the bed beside her, but it was empty, the thin cover thrown back. She scrambled out of bed and ran into the other rooms of the cottage. But there was no sign of Paul. He had awakened—if he had slept at all—some time in the night and gone home.

She was a little sobered, a little frightened. Had he, too, found her what Lisbeth had said— "inadequate as a lover"—and had he left her in disgust?

She threw on some clothes and ran down the steps and along the beach, her heart pounding hard. The door to Paul's cottage was open, she rushed in calling his name in a loud, frightened voice.

Paul, already clad in city clothes, came quickly out of the kitchen, from which now she caught the heartening smell of coffee.

"Martie, what's wrong?" he began. But before he could finish she had hurled herself into his arms so violently that he staggered a little before he could brace himself.

"Oh, Paul, I woke up and you were gone and I wondered—that is, I was afraid—" she stammered tearfully.

"Afraid? Of what, Martie?"

"That—that you didn't like me."

Paul tilted his head back and shouted with laughter.

"That I didn't like you? Hell, child, I don't. I'm just damned crazy about you," he told her, and kissed her hard and thoroughly. Now there was nothing prim nor childlike in the way she gave him back his kisses.

After a long moment, he held her a little away from him, and though there was a twinkle in his eyes, his voice was tender.

"What you really want to know is whether Lisbeth lied," he said softly. "She did, my treasure, one whopping lie, probably the biggest of her career, though that's taking in a lot of territory, for Lisbeth is one of the world's best liars."

In the delight of knowing that he had not found her an unsatisfactory lover, she scarcely noted his mention of Lisbeth, or the obvious inference that he must know Lisbeth well to be able to judge her so accurately. She only clung to him, hearing nothing beyond the fact that he was crazy about her.

"Oh, Paul, I'm so glad. Oh, Paul, you're wonderful," she told him joyously, radiantly. "I love you, too. Oh, Paul, is that coffee I smell? I'm starved."

"That's coffee you smell, and you have time for one quick cup and maybe a piece of toast and then you've got to scamper for home and into city clothes, because it's five-fifteen already and the Pine Hill bus waits for nobody."

She stood a little away from him and stared at him, roundeyed.

"You—you mean we are still going to Miami?" she stammered.

Puzzled, Paul frowned.

"Well, why not? Isn't it what we've planned?"

"But—but after last night—oh, Paul, don't you see? I don't want Jordan back; I want a divorce just as quick as I can get it, because then—well, then, Paul, you and I can always be together, like we were last night." Her voice trailed off into a miserable silence as his expression tightened a little and his eyes chilled.

"Look, honey chile," he said coaxingly after a moment, "last night was pretty wonderful, and we'll have many more nights as wonderful. But you owe it to yourself to get even with Ainslee and Lisbeth; make Ainslee pay up and plenty; take him back from Lisbeth, and make them both eat dirt. Then you and I can make our plans."

Martha stood very still, her hands clenched tightly at her sides. She had been so certain that Paul wanted her enough to marry her, now that he had found how superbly mated they were, and yet here he was just as anxious as ever to see her reconciled with Jordan! The very thought of being Jordan's wife again, of ever enduring his touch again in the intimacy of marriage. made Martha go sick and cold with repulsion.

For a moment she stood free of Paul, staring at him with wide, sick eyes. And then without a word she turned toward the door, evading Paul's outflung hand, ignoring his sharp, protesting cry of her name. She went plunging down the steps and back along the beach, and though Paul called to her again, he did not follow her.

She reached the steps of her own cottage and dropped down for a moment, both shaking hands over her white face while her breath came in hard, gasping gulps that were half-smothered sobs. She had been so bitterly hurt and humilated by Jordan and Lisbeth, and then her battered pride and self-esteem had begun to flower again beneath Paul's attentions. And last night had given her an almost arrogant self-assurance—she had been so proud and happy that she had delighted her love. But now that she had seen Paul and heard him speak, now that he had made it distressingly plain that he still wanted her to call off her divorce, to go back to Jordan, she felt as though she had been plunged into a bottomless pit into which no faintest light could fall....

She dragged herself to her feet at last and plodded up the steps and into the house. Paul had told her to get dressed to go to

Miami; dazedly she obeyed. There was no room in her jangled, chaotic thoughts for any protest. Numbly, dazedly, she was obeying orders, but nothing that could ever happen to her again could possibly hurt her as much as this.

She was dressed and putting a few things into a suitcase when a sudden blinding light burst across her numbed and bewildered consciousness. Suppose—just suppose—that Paul *did* love her. He was poor, she knew; perhaps he wanted her to get a settlement from Jordan so that she and Paul could be married! The thought gave her strength and a new, small hope.

If Paul was tired of being poor, if Paul wanted to live in the city, to have things—like well-tailored clothes, a nice apartment, a car, perhaps—well, a settlement from Jordan could guarantee all that. She was too shaken, too bitterly hurt to realize that if Paul wanted her to have wealth from Jordan so that he could share it, then Paul was by no means an admirable character. She was too far gone in her necessity to believe in Paul's need for her, in his pleasure in her, in his love, to be critical. If that was what Paul wanted—a settlement from Jordan and then a divorce— well, that made all the difference in the world, she told herself, and her shaking hands finished the job of packing.

She was on the porch, her suitcase at her feet, when Paul came striding down the beach, and his face lighted a little as he saw her outward composure. But all he said, as he swung up her suitcase, was, "All set? Then we'll have to step on it—it's almost bus time."

She nodded and trotted along behind him, finding it hard to walk in the sand in her high-heeled slippers but doing her best to keep up with Paul's long strides, though she had to make three steps to equal his one.

They made the bus merely by reason of the fact that as they came around the curve in the road the bus driver was emerging from the cafe-bus-station, and saw them as they flung up their hands in a gesture that begged him to wait. Martha hastily told the cafe proprietor to explain to Dr. Barton that she had to go to Miami and that she would write him and explain.

Now and then as they settled down to the long, rough run, Paul glanced at her uneasily, but she chatted pleasantly, coolly, of the scenery en route, and when they changed to the Miami bus at Sarasota, and had time for a real breakfast, she was determinedly gay.

Suddenly Paul put his hand on hers, smiling wryly.

"Take it easy, baby," he said softly. "You'll understand—some day. And I promise you it won't be too long."

Martha looked up at him and across the narrow table in the cafe. She said very low, "Was Lisbeth wrong?"

"Never more so in her life, Martie. You're perfect!" said Paul in tones that matched hers.

Martha nodded in solemn agreement.

"Then I think maybe I'm beginning to understand, and it's all right and I'll do exactly what you tell me," she promised him quietly.

Paul stared at her as though a little startled at the recklessness of that, but before he could say anything more their bus was announced.

CHAPTER TEN

THE TELEPHONE CALL

MIAMI IN SEPTEMBER can be hot as blazes; but then, as the irate defender of his city's incomparable perfection will demand sharply, "Where isn't it hot in September?" And it's worse than useless to argue with him. So neither Paul nor Martha tried.

After the quiet and the peace of Pine Hill, after the dilapidated, battered little houses and the blazing sun that nothing could temper, the luxury of the hotel left Martha a little dazed.

But she was only too glad to leave everything to Paul, and eventually she found herself installed in a luxurious suite on the eighth floor, overlooking the ocean, of course, with a small terrace artfully decorated with tubs of growing, blossoming plants.

And with Paul standing by, she put through a long distance call for Jordan, and sat down to wait.

"I'm a little scared, I think," she confessed to Paul.

"Nothing to be scared of," said Paul comfortingly. "I'm right here if you need me."

"I'll always need you, Paul, no matter what happens," she told him huskily.

Paul opened his mouth as though to reply, then got swiftly to his feet, jammed his hands into his pockets and walked out on the terrace, to look with unseeing eyes at the ocean.

A little later, when the telephone rang, he came back to stand watching, listening. They had gone over what she was to say, and they had even rehearsed it, so she spoke quietly, smoothly, without a trace of hesitation.

Jordan's voice sounded surprised and not unpleased to hear her voice.

"The telephone operator said Miami Beach calling—what are you doing in Miami Beach, Martie?" he asked.

"Oh, Pine Hill's a dreadful little hole and I wanted to see a bit of life," she told him gaily. "I'd never been to Miami Beach, and if I'm going to be buried in Florida in summer, I ought to see a bit of it, don't you think?"

"Yes, but leaving Pine Hill—you were supposed to stay there three months, weren't you?"

"Oh, I'll establish residence in Miami Beach; that will be a lot more fun," she assured him, gaily. "And anyway, I'm not in such a hurry about a divorce, after all."

"Oh, now, wait a minute, Martie; Lisbeth's telling all her friends—"

"Really? I didn't know she had any!" said Martha sweetly, and grinned wickedly at Paul, as though to indicate that she could ad lib if she needed to.

"You don't sound much like Martha."

"Oh, but I am. I'm still Martha, your wife, darling, and don't forget it," she assured him. "Of course, I admit I don't look much like the Martie you knew—I've 'smartened up' quite a bit, Jordan, and that's why I called you. I'm fresh out of money, so please send me some—a lot, please, because things are expensive down here."

Jordan paused as though digesting that, and when he spoke again his tone was mildly cynical.

"I see you have changed. When I offered to make a settlement, you refused it quite haughtily."

"I know—wasn't I a silly chump?" She was still gay about it. "But I've grown up, Jordy—I've grown up quite a bit. And I've grown sensible. After all, you are the one who wants the divorce, so really, don't you think you ought to be the one to pay for it? That's only fair, don't you think?"

"Of course, and that's why I offered it." Jordan was crisp and businesslike now. "How much do you need?"

"For the present, I can manage with—oh, say five thousand. You'd better wire it, Jordy, because I need it right away," she followed Paul's script literally here, though the words threatened to stick in her throat. "I'll let you know later when I need more."

She heard the small startled sound that was almost a gasp, perhaps a smothered oath, and there was a momentary hesitation before he answered.

"Well, well, well, you've certainly 'smartened up' a lot, Martie, my love." His voice was tinged with acid. "The sum of five thousand dollars would have scared you green."

"Oh, but I've learned a lot since the days at Happy Valley," she told him smoothly. "And things are expensive, and after all, I am Mrs. Jordan Ainslee. You don't want me to go around looking shabby, do you?"

"Oh, perish the thought," said Jordan piously, but there was smothered anger in his voice. "Shall I have your belongings in the apartment packed and shipped down to you?"

"Oh, goodness, no—those old rags?" She laughed blithely. "No thanks, Jordy. I'll pick up a few scraps down here. There are some wonderful sales going on. Just wire me five thousand, Jordy, and I'll let you know when I need more."

"I'll bet you will!" said Jordy grimly.

"You know I will, Jordy dear!" she told him. She put down the receiver and looked swiftly at Paul, who grinned at her and raised his hand, thumb and forefinger making a circle in a little gesture of commendation. "I don't think he liked it, Paul," she stammered faintly.

"What do you mean 'think'? You know damned well he didn't. But he doesn't despise you any more, Martie," said Paul quietly.

Martha frowned.

"Just being a bitchy little golddigger made him respect me? Paul, that sounds—well, crazy!" she protested uneasily.

"Whoever said human beings weren't crazy?" Paul pointed out mildly. "And anyway, you promised to obey orders and ask no questions. So hop to it!"

"Of course," said Martha, and avoided his eyes as she collected her hat and bag. ...

Two or three weeks later, when the apartment was strewn with new belongings and when the money Jordan had transferred for her to a local bank had shrunk incredibly, she and Paul were in the living room.

She was dressed for dinner in an airy tulle and chiffon gown that set off in its immaculate whiteness her lovely honey-tan and the smart cut of her shining, flame-colored hair. There were bits of jade glowing greenly in the lobes of her small ears, a necklace of jade about her slender throat, and on her higharched, narrow feet were slippers that had been dyed to the exact shade of the jade. Martha turned from a startled survey of herself in the full length mirror to look at Paul, puzzled.

"How do you know so much about women?" she demanded, and there was, unknown to herself, an edge of jealous resentment in her voice. "How they should do their hair, and the sort of clothes they should wear, and the way they should walk? You're a man ... "

Paul laughed, but there was a touch of new bitterness in his voice, and a cynical look in his eyes.

"You ask a question, and then answer it yourself. I'm a man, therefore I know about women. Don't you know, the study of mankind is, properly or improperly, women?" he told her, his voice a soft drawl.

"Am I beautiful now that you've finished with me?" she asked him quietly.

Paul's eyes narrowed just a little and he asked roughly, "What makes you think I'm finished with you?"

Her head went up a little, the flame-colored curls catching and imprisoning the light, and her eyes were dark, less golden-brown than black.

"I'm stupid, but not that stupid," she told him quietly. "You haven't touched me since we came to Miami Beach."

Paul turned away from her, his hands jammed into his pockets. His back looked rigid, and she watched him with tears in her eyes and her soft mouth tremulous.

"When a man paints a picture," he said over his shoulder, and his tone was taut, "he strives for perfection, and he doesn't blur that perfection by rubbing it until the paint is dry."

Martha drew a long, hard breath, but she fought down the tears and held her tongue until she could be quite sure that she could speak without her voice trembling.

"Shall we go down to dinner?" she managed then, her voice cool and stiff. "I'm starved, aren't you?"

Paul turned then and looked at her, and she saw, without wanting to, that the dark trousers of his white-jacketed dinner-clothes were shiny at the seams as though they had had long, hard service. And while his linen was immaculate it was far from new. And a little stab of pain twisted her heart. He was poor and shabby; he couldn't afford to get married. But maybe … She silenced the thought and made herself smile at him, and gathered up her jade-green bag and the silly, big square white chiffon handkerchief with the ivy-leaves delicately embroidered in one corner.

"You're the loveliest thing in the world, Martie," said Paul huskily.

She smiled radiantly at him and blinked the tears away.

"Thank you, Paul," she said. And then before she could stop herself, the words tumbled impulsively out. "Paul, if I get a whopping big settlement from Jordy, can we be married, you and I?"

Paul stared at her, his eyebrows rising almost to meet his hairline, and there was a look in his eyes that somehow sent a touch of panic through her.

"Now, what in the name of Heaven ever put *that* idea into your pretty little head?" he said a last, his tone faintly mocking. though there was an inscrutable look in his eyes.

Martha stood very still for a long moment, and then some new-found pride made it possible for her to lift her pretty shoulders above the low-cut white gown and say laughingly, "Oh, I'm the stubborn type. I go around banging my head against the wall and refusing to believe things that are so plain that anybody with a dime's-sized brain would have admitted them ages ago."

She turned toward the door with a swirl of bouffant tulle skirts and her hand was on the doorknob before he moved to follow her. And then the telephone behind them shrilled, and Paul looked at her questioningly and she made a little gesture. Paul took up the telephone.

"Yes?" she heard him say, and then saw him start and his expression alter. "Why, yes, of course, ask him to come up."

He put down the telephone and turned to Martha.

"Jordan Ainslee is in the lobby downstairs," he said flatly.

Martha cried out and leaned against the door, her eyes suddenly filled with panic.

"Jordy—here?"

"On his way up," said Paul grimly. "Do you want me to stay?"

"Oh, golly, yes!" Martha seemed as young as the day they had hunted shells on the little cay and her childish explanation matched her youth and fear. "Paul, what do you suppose he wants?"

Paul's eyes swept her in the daring, delicately lovely tulle frock, and there was a bitter look in his eyes.

"You, when he Sees the way you look now," he said dryly.

There was a knock at the door, and, startled, Martha stood away from it, and made no move to open it until the knock came the second time. Then Paul motioned to her, and stood straight, his hands deep in his pockets.

Martha drew a deep, hard breath, flung up her head and opened the door.

Jordan saw only Martha for a moment, and looked at her in startled amazement and growing delight. As he came in he took both her hands and tried to draw her into his arms.

"Well, hello!" He seemed not to notice that she was resisting his attempts to embrace her. and his eyes devoured her from head to foot. "If this is why you're overdrawn at the bank and they wired me for more funds, then I'd say it had been well spent. Martie, you're delectable."

"Oh, am I overdrawn, Jordy? I'm a rotten bookkeeper," she stammered.

"You were overdrawn, darling," laughed Jordan. "I notified them to honor your checks, but when they kept getting bigger and bigger, I decided I'd better hop down here and see what you were doing with all that money."

She turned her head and looked at Paul, while Jordan's clasp still bruised her hands, and Jordan, following her eyes, saw Paul and stiffened, his eyes blazing with anger.

"Paul Whitney!" He seemed to spit the words out in a voice that was almost a snarl. "What the hell are *you* doing here?"

"He's Paul Stephens, and he's my friend," Martha cut in.

"He's Paul Stephens Whitney, and he was Lisbeth's lover, and when she left him for me, he swore he'd get even," said Jordan through his teeth. Martha caught her breath as though she had been slapped and turned swift, dazed eyes on Paul, who smiled tightly.

"Let's not make it sound like a dishpan drama, Ainslee," said Paul grimly. "I didn't 'swear' I'd 'get even'—why should I? I was only too glad to be rid of Lisbeth."

Jordan laughed a little, but it was an ugly laugh.

"Oh, did you feel that way? Funny, then, you'd take an over-dose of sleeping pills the moment you found she'd come to me."

Paul's eyebrows went up a little.

"Oh, now, really, that's a pretty big lie for even Lisbeth to circulate—not that anyone who knows Lisbeth would believe her if she said it was a nice day, though the sun was shining bright," he said dryly.

Martha asked faintly, "Paul, is it true? Were you her lover?"

"He was, and you can take my word for it," said Jordan, and added grimly, "though I don't think even he would have the nerve to deny it."

"I don't deny it—why should I?" asked Paul reasonably, his eyes very carefully not meeting Martha's anguished regard. "Why should any of the numerous men who have enjoyed Lisbeth's favors bother to deny it? I understand that *you* are the man she intends to marry, though."

His tone so clearly added, "You poor fool!" that Martha was quite sure for a moment that the words had actually been spoken.

Jordan's face was dark with anger, but he held himself under control and looked at Martha, from the top of her lovely head to the tips of jade-green satin slippers.

"Hm-m-m, now I wonder," he drawled, and now there was a twinkle in his eyes, "how that rumor ever got about? How could I possibly marry Lisbeth, when I already have a wife? And such a lovely wife!"

Once more he tried to draw Martha into his arms, but she drew away from him, her head held high, her eyes frosty.

"Oh, but I'm down here to divorce you—remember?" she told him icily. "By your own orders—remember that, too, please."

Jordan laughed and shook his handsome head.

"Those orders have been canceled, as of the moment I stepped through the door and looked at you. Oh, no, my pretty—you're not going to divorce me! I'm not letting you get away from me again!" he told her firmly.

Paul said, before Martha could speak, "If you will excuse me … "

"It'll be a pleasure," said Jordan happily and obligingly swung open the door, standing beside it, his hand on the knob, his manner one of such arrogant ease and such command of the situation that Martha set her teeth hard.

"Paul," she said huskily, "Paul, don't go."

"Martie, darling," protested Jordan, with a little caressing laugh.

Paul moved toward the door, and there he paused for a moment and looked straight into Jordan's excited, laughing eyes.

"All right, Ainslee, you've got her back again; now see that you take care of her," he said evenly. "For I'm warning you, if I ever get another chance with her—"

"You won't," said Jordan arrogantly. "You'd better run along and console Lisbeth. I'll look after Martie!"

"See that you do," Paul went out, his shoulders very straight, and if he heard Martha's little crying of his name he gave no indication.

When the door had closed behind him, Jordan came swiftly to Martha, but she evaded him when he would have taken her into his arms, and he looked hurt.

"Look, angel," he coaxed. Once that warm, caressing murmur would have been like small, deft fingers playing on the very strings of her heart and would have turned her will to water so that he could have done anything he wanted with her, but now it left her cold. "I know I treated you shamefully, and I'll get down and let you walk on me, and set the marks of your little high heels all over my neck, if it will help to win your forgiveness. But after all, Martie, how did I know you could look like this? You didn't, before."

Martha said thinly, "It's the dress."

Jordan leaned on the back of the chair that she had moved between them and studied her and shook his head.

"It's not the clothes," he told her firmly, and the puzzlement grew in his eyes. "I bought you beautiful clothes, and you had everything the beauty shops, even the finest of them, could do, but you didn't look like this. Oh, you were lovely, of course, but you were—well, a lovely child. Like a luscious fruit not quite ripe. A little tart to the taste, but promising one day—and now the promise is fulfilled."

He paused for a long, long moment and then his jaw hardened.

"How long have you known Whitney?" he demanded unexpectedly.

She tilted her pretty chin defiantly and her eyes were cold.

"Ever since I came to Florida," she answered him frankly.

Jordan's eyes narrowed.

"Is he your lover?"

Martha's color deepened but her eyes remained hostile, meeting his own straightly, coolly.

"I shall not answer that because it's a question you have no right to ask," she told him coolly.

"You're my wife."

"Not any more."

"The divorce is off, Martie."

"Oh, no it isn't!" she flashed hotly. "Do you think for one moment I'd live with you again?"

He was startled at the sudden disgust in her tone, and his eyes narrowed a little.

"So Whitney is your lover, damn him," he said softly. "Well, we'll put a stop to that! You're going back to New York with me."

"I'll do nothing of the sort."

Jordan was angry, but after a moment he forced himself to speak in that gentle, coaxing voice that once had had such power to charm her.

"Look, sweet, we've made a mess of things," he said tenderly. "I admit the whole thing was my fault from the very beginning. I married you because Lisbeth dared me to—I may as well admit it. Oh, I was crazy about you and you were cute and sweet and it had been years since I'd known a virgin. Then I lost you because I didn't have sense enough to appreciate you. Give me another chance, Martie, and I'll prove I can make you happy. You loved me once, Martie, and you're not the sort of girl to turn love on and off like an electric light switch."

In spite of herself, Martha was shaken. She *had* loved him, desperately. So much that when he and Lisbeth had stood before her that night and proclaimed that they belonged to each other, the whole world had seemed to crash before her. She had fought her way out of that blackness through Paul's friendship. Friendship? Dared she use a stronger word?

Her mind went back to that enchanted night in the dilapidated cottage at Pine Hill, when in Paul's arms her whole being had flowered into an ecstasy beyond anything she had ever dreamed possible. But had that been love? Paul had taken her, it was true, but only because she had practically thrust herself on him. Paul had not in any way at all indicated that he cared for her. He had merely accepted the gift of herself, thrust upon him in such a way that it had been almost impossible for him to refuse it—just as any man in his position would have done. And she had not the faintest scrap of reason for believing that he cared for her.

Jordan had said that Paul had sworn to avenge himself for losing Lisbeth; he had from the first planned on bringing her and Jordan together again, leaving Lisbeth high and dry, but never for a moment had Paul indicated that he cared for Martha. Knowing now that he had been Lisbeth's lover, that she had left him for Jordan, it all became blindingly clear. Paul's presence at Pine Hill had not been accidental; he had known she was going there—perhaps he had followed her. Perhaps Beelzy had told him. All of it had been planned deliberately, for the single purpose of avenging himself on Lisbeth; perhaps his hope was to get Lisbeth back!

Jordan said after a moment, his tone edged with anger, "Martie, you're not listening. What's the matter?"

She pulled herself together and lifted her head.

"I'm sorry, Jordy."

"I was saying, Martie, that if you'll come back to New York with me—"

"No, Jordy, not as your wife!"

"All right, then, I'll get you an apartment of your own. I'll pretend we've just met, and I'll woo you all over again," said Jordan, and laughed a little. "Come to think of it, we sort of overlooked the usual courtship stage in our marriage, didn't we? But come back, Martie, and have your own apartment, and I'll send you flowers, and take you to dinner and to parties, and buy you pretty presents—I'll behave like any young man wildly in love. And Martie, difficult as it will be, I won't ask anything of you until you are quite sure that you're in love with me. I won't expect you actually to be my wife until you are as eager for it as I am! There, now! Who could ask for a fairer arrangement than that?"

Martha was tired and shaken and bewildered, and the fact that she had had no dinner and that the thought of food made her ill all added to her understandable mental confusion.

"I—I'll think about it, Jordy," she told him at last, merely to get rid of him, for she had to be alone for a little while or she would go into hysterics. "I want to be alone now, and think about things."

Jordan said huskily, and there was in his eyes a flame that had scorched her and left her dazed and shaken, "Martie, you're so lovely. How can I leave you, when you look like that? Come and have dinner with me, Martie—we'll go somewhere and dance, and I'll begin my courtship. You owe me that, surely."

And because it was less effort to go with him than to keep on arguing, Martha gave in.

Jordan was obviously pleased and delighted to be recognized by the head waiter as they entered the dining room.

"It's a pleasure to see you again, Mr. Ainslee," said the man with the obvious manner of one who confidently expects a sizable tip.

"Thanks, Jules," said Jordan happily. "I hope you've been taking good care of my wife?"

He beamed expansively at Martha, who flushed and looked away.

"It's been a privilege, sir," said Jules handsomely, and snapped his fingers soundlessly toward a waiter, who came scurrying.

As Jordan went into a conference over the menu with the waiter attending him devotedly, Martha looked about the room and her eyes caught and were held by Paul's. He sat across the room at the table where he and Martha had sat so often. And as her eyes found him, he grinned and lifted his hand, thumb and forefinger making a neat circle in a sort of congratulatory gesture that made Martha set her teeth hard and turn her head away from him, lest even at that distance he suspect the tears in her eyes.

CHAPTER ELEVEN
THE TRUTH ABOUT PAUL

JORDAN SET THE pace for the evening, and it was very gay, and she worked hard at pretending to be amused and happy about the whole thing. But when he brought her back to her suite in the mid-dawn and attempted to draw her into his arms, she evaded him, her jaw set.

"No, Jordy, no!" she told him swiftly.

"Not even so much as a tiny good-night kiss?" pleaded Jordan.

"I'm sorry, Jordy."

"You don't forgive very easily, do you?" Jordan complained, and then with an almost visible effort he resumed his coaxing, conciliatory tone. "All right, sweet, I'll be good. I promised you a whale of a courtship and ample time to make up your mind about me. But you're still my wife, sweet, and don't forget it For I'm not going to."

She closed the door behind him and clung to it for a moment, her hands over her face. It was all so crazy, so silly. Once she had thrilled to the touch of Jordan's hands, to his kiss; she had ached with longing for him. Yet now that he was hers again for the taking, the very thought of surrendering her body to him turned her sick with revulsion.

She beat her palms soundlessly together as she walked up and down the room, so shaken, so troubled, so miserable that she could think of nothing, of nobody but Paul. And that was wild and crazy, for she had told Paul she loved Jordan and wanted him back, and Paul had told her he could get Jordan back for her. Well, now he had, and she no longer wanted Jordan; she wanted Paul. Face it, she told herself furiously; face it, and admit what a shameless wanton you are. Going from one man to another and always wanting the last!

Paul!

The name seemed to stand forth in her mind in letters of rose and blue and gold. With Paul everything would always be gloriously right. And without him—the very thought shook her to the depths of her being and suddenly, almost without being aware of what she was doing, and despite the hour, which was close to four A.M., she caught up the telephone. And when a sleepy clerk spoke in her ear, she asked harshly for Paul's room.

"I'm sorry, Mrs. Ainslee," said the sleepy voice politely after a moment, "but the gentleman checked out early in the evening."

Martha stood holding the telephone for a long moment before she eased the receiver back in its cradle as though it had been something very fragile that might easily break. And after a long, long time, when the sun was already lifting above the horizon, she went to bed and hid her face in the pillow, and lay very still.

It was noon before the telephone awoke her. It was Jordan, saying with warm tenderness. "Hello, sleepyhead—a darned nuisance having to telephone to wake you up. How do you feel? Like a swim before breakfast? In the hotel pool, of course."

"Why not?" said Martha, and set her teeth hard when she had put the telephone down.

Well, after all, why not? She had what she had said she wanted. She had Jordan back; and she could do anything with him she wanted—except, she corrected herself dryly, get rid of him! For Jordan always wanted most that which was difficult to get. He had never yet admitted there was anything he couldn't have, if he wanted it enough. She could remember many instances in their brief married life when an object he had casually desired, being denied him, had immediately become the one thing in the world he *had* to have; and sometimes the ruthlessness of his fight for whatever it was had appalled her a little. He had always been rich; he had been spoiled; he had been taught that the world was his oyster; he had learned the lesson well.

She slid out of bed and looked at herself in the mirror. But if she had expected to see some sign of the bitter pain of losing Paul, of being made to realize that she had never really *had* him, she was disappointed. She was radiantly lovely, and she turned away from the mirror, her teeth set hard in her lower lip, her eyes bitter.

But when she met Jordan beside the oblong turquoise beauty of the hibiscus framed pool, in the brief French bathing suit Paul had insisted she buy, she was outwardly cool and selfoossessed.

Jordan's eves flamed as she dropped her terry-cloth beach wrao on a long canvas-covered cabana-chair, and instinctively his hands reached for her as she dived into the pool. A moment later he had dived, and as they rose together to the brilliant sunlight, he said hoarsely, "Martie, you're glorious! But I don't think I approve of that suit!" he told her sternly.

Martha laughed.

"It's almost exactly like the one you made me wear—remember?" she drawled as she swam toward the edge of the pool.

"I know, but somehow you look different in this one," complained Iordan, as they reached the edge of the pool and pulled themselves up on the edge. "You looked like a kid in that one. You've blossomed. Martie."

Her eyes mocked him as she tugged the cap from her head and shook out her glowing curls.

"Are you trying to say I've grown fat, Jordy?"

"Oh, perish the thought!" Jordan was shocked. "It's just as though you'd grown up."

Suddenly he stiffened a little and his eyes blazed.

"I'd hate to think Paul Whitney had anything to do with this sudden blossoming," he said harshly.

She had schooled herself to hearing Paul's name without visibly wincing, but she turned her head away so that he could not see the look in her eyes.

"Paul's been most helpful," she said thinly, and could have burst into wild, hysterical laughter at the inadequacy of the word.

"Oh, he's quite a guy, I suppose," said Jordan grimly. "And if he helped you select the clothes I've seen you wear, and the new hair-do, which is cute as the dickens and makes a new woman out of you—well, then I'm indebted to him, damn him! Of course a man in his line would know a hell of a lot about how a woman could make the most of her looks. After all, he's one of the best-known and highest-priced portrait painters in the country. Women who can afford his fees, and a lot of them that can't, scramble like mad to get him to put them on canvss."

The last of Martha's tiny hopes died. She had thought Paul poor; she had thought that he loved her, maybe, and that if she got a whopping big settlement from Jordan ... But now that she knew that Paul was rich, that he earned enormous sums, she had to believe only that he had befriended her in order to free Lisbeth for himself. He had been Lisbeth's lover; he must love her still. But to get her away from Jordan, in view of Jordan's wealth and power, he had just had to get Jordan back for Martha.

The last tiny bit of the jig-saw puzzle slipped into place and it was all so terribly clear that she flinched a little before it. That night at the cottage when she had begged him to stay with her, when she had forced herself upon him, he had wanted her no more than any normal man wants any desirable woman. And he *had* said that she was desirable.

She drew a deep, hard breath and lifted her young chin proudly. Well, she'd got over Jordan; she could get over Paul. And she was young—and desirable—her mouth twisted a little at that reminder—and the world was full of men.

"I don't now how long I'm going to be able to trust myself, Martie," said Jordan softly, and his voice was a little rough and his eyes were clinging to her with a look that made her shrink inwardly. "Either you'd better go and put some clothes on, or the hotel is going to be shocked out of its dignity by the sight of a man hurling his tempting wife to the ground and—"

She made herself laugh at him and scrambled to her feet and she flung her beach wrap about her with a mocking little gesture of modesty as she danced out of his reach.

"A man making public love to his own wife—oh, I'm sure everybody in the hotel would be shocked speechless," she told him mockingly. "And we must protect the hotel's dignity. Meet you for breakfast in half an hour."

"You'd better, or I'll batter down your door," Jordan told her as she laughed and ran away from him ...

When, a day or two later, he suggested that they should return to New York, she saw no reason to refuse. Paul had been gone since Jordan's arrival, and there was nothing to hold her here. She had given up the idea of divorcing Jordan.

Jordan suggested, "What about your stuff at Pine Hill? Shall we drive over and pick it up?"

Martha's heart twisted a little, and then her mouth thinned and she shook her head.

"There's nothing there worth bothering about," she told him. "I'll write to Dr. Barton and ask him to have it packed for me and keep it for me."

She slanted a deliberately provocative eye at him and finished, "Then if I decide again that I want a divorce, it will be there waiting for me."

Jordan caught her hand across the breakfast table and held it tightly, his eyes hot and demanding.

"You'll never decide again you want a divorce, Martie. I won't let you?" he told her, and his voice was harsh and passionate. "I've promised to give you plenty of time to fall in love with me all over again; but, Martie, be merciful, darling—don't make me wait very long. I want you so damnably."

Martha studied him curiously, almost as though he had been someone she had never seen before, someone she wasn't quite sure she liked. And then she freed her hand to take a cigarette from the case on the table, and bent its tip to the match Jordan offered instantly.

"I have to be sure, Jordan," she told him then, her voice cool, level, her manner poised. "Down here, where we are more or less alone, you think you want me again—"

"Think, she says," Jordan groaned savagely. "Damn it, you are innocent."

Her smile was thin and cool.

"Not any more, Jordy, but let it pass," she went on. "I'll have to see how you behave when we are back in New York, among your usual distractions."

"If you mean Lisbeth—"

"And all the other Lisbeths who have come and gone, and will come."

His jaw set a little.

"There are times when I don't recognize you at all, Martie," he complained. "Times when you seem much too old and too wise and disturbingly cynical."

Martha's smile did not deepen, nor did it acquire any trace of mirth.

"Remember, I've grown up," she told him mildly. "You said so yourself."

Jordan nodded, and studied her curiously.

"You're more beautiful, but you're—well, you're almost hard, Martie."

"Do you find that hard to understand?"

He flushed a little and faced her squarely.

"Frankly, no. I've given you a very raw deal," he admitted. "The least I could have done was to have told you myself that I wanted a divorce. To bring Lisbeth along, and to let her spit out her ugly lies—"

Martha's eyes widened a little.

"Oh, they were lies?"

Puzzled, Jordan stared at her.

"I don't quite get you, Martie. She said that we were in love, and I suppose, at the time, we thought we were."

"And that I was unsatisfactory as a lover."

Jordan's eyes flamed and his hands reached for her, despite the fact that they were by no means alone in the big hotel dining room.

"That, Martie, was the most barefaced lie any living creature ever spoke," he told her huskily.

"I'm glad to hear that," Martha drawled coolly. "It hurt more than somewhat. No girl, even as young and stupid as I was, likes to think a thing like that of herself."

"Saying that to you is, I think, the most unforgivable thing Lisbeth ever said in her life."

"Since it happens to be something no woman could know about another woman, unless some man told her—" Martha delivered her thrust quietly, yet with deadly force.

Jordan's eyes were wide now and his jaw was a set, angry line.

"No, Martie, no. You couldn't believe a thing like that of me —not even after the way I've behaved. You can't believe that I ever said such a thing."

Martha nodded, and there was a trace of warmth in her eyes.

"Lisbeth knew it was the one thing that would hurt most, so, being Lisbeth, that was what she said," she told him quietly. "I know, of course, that it isn't true."

Jordan's eyes sharpened a little.

"Oh, you do, do you? And may I ask how you learned?" he demanded sharply.

She only laughed and thrust back her chair and said coolly, "If we're to take the four-thirty plane for New York, I'd better do something about packing. I really have something to pack this time—you're sweet, Jordy, and you're very generous, and I'm grateful."

"Thanks," said Jordan grimly, "thanks one hell of a lot for practically nothing."

She laughed back at him over her shoulder and went out of the room, moving with the light-footed, unself-conscious grace of all young and perfectly coordinated creatures, while Jordan stood at the table, oblivious to the hovering waiter, and watched her until the elevator had swallowed her up.

CHAPTER TWELVE

SO NEAR, SO FAR

THE FIRST PERSON they saw when they came from the plane was Beelzy. He stood waiting for them, a short, stocky, ugly little man in a loud checked suit, and as she met his eyes, Martha lifted her chin just a little. For she had promised herself since the moment she had decided to come back that she would take no nonsense from Beelzy. Once she had been secretly more than a little afraid of him; but now she felt in complete command of the situation, and as though he sensed that, Beelzy dropped his eyes after one swift glance at her.

"Hello, Beelzy," she said coolly. "I hope you've been well?"

Beelzy shot her a swift glance, a flicker of the eyes toward Jordan, and then he shuffled his feet a little.

"Oh, sure, sure, I'm in the pink, like always. Me, I'm never sick," he assured her.

"Isn't that nice?" purred Martha sweetly, and though there was nothing wrong with the words or her tone, Beelzy seemed to squirm just a little inside his loud checked suit.

"I done like you said, boss." He turned to Jordan with obvious relief. "I got the da—the lady a suite at a apartment hotel. It was the best I could do. Maybe you don't know it, but they's a housing shortage in N'Yawk."

"I have heard rumors," Jordan agreed, and turned anxiously to Martha. "Sure you wouldn't rather come home, darling?"

STUDENT NURSE

"Quite sure, thank you," Martha told him composedly. "The hotel will be very nice. I'm sure Beelzy found a nice one and I'll be very comfortable there. After Pine Hill, I don't care much about any domestic facilities. I'm going to enjoy a hotel. It was fun at Miami Beach, and I'm sure it will be here."

Beelzy eyed her and then Jordan; before the look in Jordan's eyes, Beelzy's fell and he said hurriedly, "The car's over here, boss."

Jordan drew Martha's hand through his arm with a loverlike gesture Beelzy's little close-set eyes did not miss and led the way. In the big car, rolling smoothly toward town, Martha smiled at Jordan and said lightly, "I think New York is going to be fun, don't you?"

"It's going to be a mess of hard work for me for a while, but I'll try to see to it that you're not bored or lonely," he promised her warmly.

She slid her hand out of his carelessly, and laughed.

"Oh, you musn't have me on your mind while you're putting a new show together, darling," she drawled gaily.

To her startled amazement, Jordan's hands caught her by the shoulders and jerked her about until she was facing him on the wide, luxuriously cushioned seat, and his face was white with anger beneath its recently acquired suntan.

"Don't call me 'darling' in that gay little tone you'd use to speak to a—a damned little Pekinese!" he said through his teeth. "I won't have it! I'm in love with you; I'm crazy about you; I won't have you using the same tone, the same endearment to me that you use to a salesgirl in a shop, a friendly pup, a woman you loathe and despise. Stop short-changing me! Do you hear?"

Martha drew herself from his arms and faced him with her chin up, her eyes cold.

"I hear you," she said icily. "And I imagine Beelzy does, too. Or does that matter, since he is practically your other self? I'm sorry if I disturbed you with my endearments. You may be quite sure that in the future I shall be more careful, Jordan."

Jordan locked his hands tightly together between his knees, and turned his head away from her, his jaw ridged.

"Sorry I blew my top," he said unevenly. "It's just that I'm not used to being denied something the way I want you."

"I tried to tell you, Jordan, that it would be much better if we went ahead with the divorce."

"That way, I'd really go to pieces!" he cut in grimly. "I don't know what kind of 'black magic' you've invoked against me; you're the first woman I've ever known who's really put me over the ropes. I've known more beautiful women; I've known more seductive, more sophisticated women. I could take 'em or leave 'em—and usually managed to do both, one after the other. But you've got under my skin as no other woman has ever been able to do, and I don't like it! Because I don't understand it."

"Don't you, Jordan? It's very simple," she said quietly. "I'm the first woman who has ever said 'no' to you."

He nodded grimly.

"I suppose so," he admitted wryly. "But I'll wind up back at that elegantly appointed and painfully expensive booby-hatch known as Happy Valley if I lose you—and that I know for sure!"

She was disturbed, more than a little uneasy.

"Jordan, I made no promises—I don't make any now—I don't know whether I can ever love you again," she stammered.

"You will," he told her, and now he was eagerly confident again. And when he clutched both her hands in his. though she winced, she made no effort to withdraw them. "I'm going to make you love me, Martie."

"Oh, Jordan," she whispered helplessly, and there were tears in her eyes and a new, creeping uneasiness in her heart. After all, what was she doing? She was appalled at the thought of Jordan's hunger for her, which only her own desire could satisfy. It would do no good to yield to him unless she could satisfy his need for her. And only her own active desire could do that. The very thought was frightening, and she wished devoutly that she had stayed at Pine Hill and gone through with the divorce and never seen him again. How many times and how devoutly she was to wish that in the next few weeks she had no way of knowing. Which was perhaps just as well!

The hotel was smart, the address "good," and when the car came to a halt before it, Jordan looked up at its facade, and nodded approvingly at Beelzy, who looked relieved.

Beelzy led to the way to the elevator, two bell-hops struggling with the small sea of luggage behind them, and on the fourteenth floor, Beelzy put a key in the lock, turned the knob and stood back.

Martha led the way in, and the first thing that met her eyes were vast quantities of flowers. They were everywhere, in huge florists' baskets, in bowls, in vases.

"I thought I'd pretty up the joint a little with some posies," Beelzy explained anxiously at Jordan's startled frown.

"And that you did, Beelzy my lad, that you did," said Jordan acidly.

Beelzy looked hurt.

"Well, I thought it would make the dump look homelike," he protested.

Martha took pity on him, as Jordan tipped the bell-hops.

"And it does look nice, Beelzy," she told him swiftly, and smiled at him. "I love flowers and these are beautiful."

"We'll have 'em dumped at the nearest hospital," said Jordan as he closed the door behind the happy bell-hops.

"We'll do nothing of the kind," protested Martha warmly. "They are my flowers and I am going to keep them. Beelzy and I are going to be friends this time, aren't we, Beelzy?"

Beelzy looked embarrassed but pleased, and when she put out her hand he thrust his own out to meet it, and then hastily withdrew it.

"No judo?"

"Of course not, Beelzy—and anyway, I'm all out of practice," Martha laughed.

"Gee, you hadn't ought to let yourself get out o' practice," protested Beelzy with professional horror. "That was one sweet little job you done on me, and I ain't kiddin'."

"Oh, well, I guess I could still defend myself if I had to, even if I am a little rusty," laughed Martha, and Jordan jerked his head toward the door, dismissing Beelzy.

Martha tensed a little as the door closed behind him, and she and Jordan were alone. Jordan looked about the suite; the living room with its absurd banking of flowers, the large, beautifully appointed bedroom with its twin beds, the bath, the tiny kitchenette and serving pantry at the opposite end of the living room.

"Think you can be comfortable here, Martie?" he asked at last. "Sure you won't feel cramped? It's about a third as large as my apartment, you know."

"Cramped, after Pine Hill?" she laughed. "Oh, Jordy, you should have seen that. This is luxury beyond words."

"You didn't have to go and live like that, Martie."

"Yes, I did, Jordy," she cut in quietly. "I had to wake up. To grow up."

Jordan's eyes swept over her, kindling with that flame she was beginning to dread.

"Then I can't complain if Pine Hill is what did this to you," he said eagerly. "You're a new woman, Martie, and a lovely one."

"And at the moment, a very tired one, Jordy, so if you don't mind I'm going to ask you to run along now," she told him gaily.

He hesitated for a moment, and looked beyond her to the open door of the bedroom.

"There's plenty of room here for two," he hinted.

"Oh, no, there isn't. You just said yourself I might be cramped," she reminded him, trying not to let him see the tiny thrill of revulsion that shook her at the thought of sharing this place, or any place, with him.

For a moment she saw the old, sullen, stubborn look on his face and his eyes glinted. But then he got himself under control and bade her goodnight almost brusquely. She closed the door behind him and turned the key in the lock, panting a little as though she had been running.

She was frightened of what she had done in coming back with Jordan, and yet she could not quite see what else she could have done. And suddenly, without the slightest intention of doing such a thing, she went into the bedroom, took up the telephone directory, and opened it to the "W" listing. She ran her finger down the column until she came to "Whitney, Paul S." and the number following it. For a long moment she sat very still looking down at the name and her hand hovered over the telephone, but she made herself stop. Paul was here, only a few blocks away, no farther away than her telephone; yet for all that he could mean to her, he might be worlds and oceans away. The thought was a lonely whimpering in her heart, and in spite of herself tears came.

Suddenly she jerked herself to her feet, her eyes stormy, and began scolding herself furiously.

"Face it and behave yourself, Martie, you fool," she said under her breath, her voice acid. "Paul wants Lisbeth, not you. You forced yourself on him, and he took you—any man under the same circumstances would. But Paul's through with you, so for Pete's sake, try to dredge up a few scraps of pride and face it! You're young and there are a lot of years ahead of you; and the sooner you make up your mind to admit that Paul's lost to you— if you can lose something you never had, which I doubt—and try to figure some way to go on living and make the best of it, the better off you'll be."

It was brave talk, and it helped. A little. Not much. But she set herself to the task of unpacking, of putting away her belongings, and then she soaked in a warm relaxing bath and finally went to bed. But it was a long time before sleep came to her.

CHAPTER THIRTEEN
LISBETH GETS A PLAN

S HE WAS AWAKENED by the Jangling of the telephone bell, and when she put out a sleepy hand to it, the hotel clerk said politely, "Good morning, Mrs. Ainslee. Miss Lisbeth Harlow is calling."

"On the telephone?"

"No, Mrs. Ainslee, she's here in the lobby."

For just a moment Martha hesitated, and then a light of battle dawned in her eyes and she said crisply, "Please ask Miss Harlow to give me fifteen minutes and then send her up."

She slid out of bed and into her shower. She searched her wardrobe for the most seductive negligee she had brought with her. She wrapped its leaf-green chiffon over the frail tea-rose pink of her nightie. She started to apply makeup, and then saw how fresh and scrubbed and glowing her face looked without it, and chuckled. Instead she used a geranium pink lipstick, grinned a little, called Room Service and ordered her breakfast.

Before she had finished, there was a knock at the door and she went briskly to open it, to reveal Lisbeth standing there, beautifully groomed, very lovely, and obviously in a towering rage.

"Why, Lisbeth, darling, how very nice of you to welcome me home—and so early, too!" purred Martha sweetly. "I know eleven in the morning is practically the middle of the night to you theatrical people."

Lisbeth's eyes blazed as she stepped into the suite, and she looked at Martha from head to foot, missing nothing of the young, exquisite curves of Martha's body revealed by the fragile wisps of chiffon.

"Do sit down, darling," said Martha sweetly, "I've ordered breakfast and we'll have some coffee. I could certainly use some, couldn't you?"

"I could, if yours had a dash of cyanide in it," said Lisbeth savagely.

Martha made her eyes very wide and round, even though she laughed.

"Why, darling," she began in a tone of sweet wonder.

"Let's skip the cute and airy chatter, shall we?" said Lisbeth through her teeth. "It's all I can do to keep my hands off you as it is, and one more '*dahling*!' from you will just about be more than I can take!"

"Really?" Martha's tone was cool and amused. "It was you who came calling, remember? I didn't send for you, you know."

Lisbeth ground out a most unladylike oath between her teeth and then she asked thinly, "Just what the hell are you up to? That's all I want to know!"

Once more Martha's eyes were round and puzzled.

"I'm afraid I don't understand," she began.

"Wipe that baby-faced innocence off your silly-looking face, and save it for them as will believe it, because I most certainly won't," Lisbeth cut in shortly. "You went off to get a divorce from Jordy—fine and dandy. Then all of a sudden Jordy dashes off pell-mell to Miami Beach where you weren't supposed to be at all, and now he tells me that the divorce is off—so where does that leave me?"

"Out in the cold, I'd say, wouldn't you?" suggested Martha gently.

"And you think I'm going to stay there?"

"Well, I really don't see what else you can do, do you?"

Martha's tone was so sweetly reasonable that Lisbeth's hands clenched tightly into hard fists and her mouth was a thin, ugly line. But before she could speak there was a knock at the door and the waiter came in with breakfast.

Lisbeth sat perfectly still, smoking, watching Martha as she tipped the waiter and dismissed him. Martha drew her chair up to the table, whisked a napkin across her lap, and lifted the tall, slender coffeepot invitingly above the extra cup.

"I ordered coffee for you, too—shall I pour it?" she suggested, the courteous, gracious hostess.

"Why not?" said Lisbeth grimly, and scrubbed out her cigarette and reached for the coffee. "We might as well be civilized about this."

"By al! means, let's be civilized," agreed Martha warmly.

Lisbeth stirred her coffee thoughtfully, her eyes never leaving Martha's face. She noted with smothered anger and jealousy the youthful, scrubbed face guiltless of makeup save for the light lipstick, and felt suddenly- old and heavily made-up. The feeling shook her badly and deepened her hatred of this girt.

"How much?" she asked suddenly, her tone harsh.

Martha looked at her, lightly surprised.

"My dear Lisbeth, are you trying to buy me off? Let's not be 'dish-pan drama-ish.' " But her lightness shook a little as the memory came flashing back of Paul using almost that same expression to Jordan that night when Jordan had arrived in Miami Beach.

"All right, if you don't want money, then what the hell *do* you want?" snapped Lisbeth, and set the coffee cup down so roughly that the milky-brown liquid slopped over into the saucer. "Why, after telling Jordy that you wanted no part of him or his money either, did you suddenly call up demanding large sums of money? And now why have you come back here, without getting a divorce? Why?"

"Because Jordy asked me to," said Martha quietly.

That was, of course, a blow in the face to Lisbeth, and her eyes widened a little.

"I don't believe you," she said harshly.

"I don't imagine you'll find it easy to, so I'd suggest you talk to Jordy about it," said Martha.

"Don't think I won't!" Lisbeth exploded savagely.

Martha looked up at her, a little puzzled.

"You haven't seen Jordy since he—since we came back?"

"No. That baboon, Beelzy, won't let me into the apartment, and when I call Beelzy answers the telephone and says "The boss is busy.' I know there's some kind of shenanigans going on, but just what it is—" Lisbeth set her teeth hard and her hand shook a little as she selected a cigarette and managed to get it alight.

Martha sat very still for a moment and when she looked up at Lisbeth, she was genuinely sorry for her and the pity was in her eyes for Lisbeth to see.

"Lisbeth, do you love Jordan very much?" she asked softly.

Lisbeth's eyes widened, and her anger at Martha's pity was swallowed up momentarily in contempt for the silliness of such a question.

"You poor little damned fool kid!" she drawled savagely. "That's exactly the sort of question I'd expect from a little sap like you. Love! *Bah!*"

Martha relaxed a little and leaned back, pouring more coffee for herself, and saying lightly in a tone of deep relief, "Oh, well, then, that's all right. If you were terribly in love with Jordy, I'd feel badly about his changing his mind about wanting to marry you—because he has, you know. But if you're not in love with him—"

She ended the sentence with a little shrug and sipped at her coffee, her smile sunny and sweet.

Lisbeth stared at her for a long moment, and then she scrubbed out her cigarette, her hand shaking a little, and leaned toward Martha.

"I intend to marry Jordan Ainslee, and you may as well get that straight in what passes for that silly little mind of yours! If you're in love with him, as you call it, then that's just too damned bad for you."

"Oh, but I'm not," Martha assured her quickly.

Lisbeth looked puzzled.

"Then why the hell—" she began furiously.

"Because *he's* in love with *me*; it's very simple," said Martha.

For a moment Lisbeth was still, and then her lovely mouth twisted into an ugly line and her eyes were bitter.

"And of course you are holding him up for every penny you can get and then you'll step aside and I can marry him."

"I don't think you can, not really," Martha interrupted her gently. "As soon as you see him and talk to him—" She broke off and frowned. "And incidentally, if you haven't seen him, how did you know I was back and that the divorce plans had been cancelled?"

"I read the Broadway gossip columnists—don't you?" Lisbeth's tone was dry and bitter.

"Why, no." Martha's eyes widened a little. "You mean they are writing things about me?"

"Don't let your head swell pal! Not about you as you, but about you as Jordan Ainslee's wife. They are wondering why the divorce plans are off, and if they are off, why you are here instead of in the Ainslee penthouse. And so am I, baby, so am I!"

Martha hesitated for a moment, and then she lifted her head and her eyes met Lisbeth's straightly.

"For the gossip columnists, Lisbeth, I'm here because Jordan's putting together a new show and the penthouse is a madhouse when that's going on, as you know," she said evenly. "But between you and me, I do feel you have the right to know the truth. Which is that Jordy begged me to give him another chance to—to—well, to try to get me to fall in love with him again."

Lisbeth stared at her in amazed disbelief.

"Well, I'll be damned!" she said very softly.

Martha, watching her, felt she could see the other woman's thoughts, read her mind, and so she said quietly, "But I don't think you can get him back again."

"You mean you are in love with him again?"

Martha shook her bright head.

"No, I'm almost sure now that I never was," she admitted honestly. "I think I was in love with love, and Jordy sort of bowled me over, and before I knew what it was all about, I was married to him."

"He was never in love with you for a minute—he married you to spite me," said Lisbeth hotly.

Martha nodded soberly.

"Because you'd been double-crossing him with Paul," she said quietly. "That's why I think that even if I can't learn to love Jordy, you won't be able to get him back. He still holds that against you. He hates Paul."

Lisbeth was listening tautly, frowning a little.

"Paul?" she repeated. "Do you mean Whit? Paul Whitney? What do you know about him?"

Martha's face twisted a little and grew hot. She hated herself for blushing, but could not control it, though her eyes met Lisbeth's straightly.

"I met Paul in Florida," she said painfully.

For a long moment, Lisbeth stared at her, narrow-eyed, a wicked gleam in her eyes.

"So you met Paul," she said very softly, "and now you're in love with him."

She spoke so softly that for a full moment Martha did not try to answer; it was almost as though she was not quite sure what Lisbeth had said. And then the soft color died in her lovely face and her head went up.

"That's got nothing to do with anything," she said swiftly. "Paul's still in love with you, Lisbeth—that's why he helped me get Jordy back—so that *he* could have you again."

Lisbeth's eyes widened a little, and then she chuckled.

"You don't say!" she drawled sweetly, malice filling her eyes. "You don't say! Well, well, well, this is interesting! So you're madly in love with Whit, and no doubt Whit had more than a little to do with all this sudden transformation that has taken place in you! I'd never have believed that taking a lover could make such a difference. I must try it sometime."

"Again, you mean, don't you? But I understand that after a certain age the results are not so certain," said Martha through her teeth.

Lisbeth's eyes flashed, but she controlled herself and stood up, confident, laughing a little.

"Poor Jordy. First his girl friend two-times him with Paul Whitney, and now his wife. I wonder what Jordy will say to that when I tell him," she purred, as sweetly malicious as Martha had been when Lisbeth first arrived.

"He knows," said Martha quietly.

That stopped Lisbeth in her tracks, halfway to the door, and she turned to stare incredulously at Martha, who nodded.

"He knows," Martha repeated. "He guessed, and I didn't deny it."

"And yet he brought you back here with him? I don't believe it!" flared Lisbeth violently.

Martha's smile was slight, but it somehow stung Lisbeth.

"Then you don't know Jordy very well, Lisbeth," she said quietly. "He never wants anything very much until he finds that someone else wants the same thing. And then he *has* to have it, no matter what it costs."

Lisbeth leaned against the door frame staring at Martha, her airy brows drawn together in a little frown of concentration.

"Hm-m-m!" she mused softly, her eyes on space. "He didn't particularly want to do Bellamy's play, but when he found that Soperman was anxious to produce it...and when Sara Dulaine was suggested for a part, he refused until he found out that she had a good offer from Hollywood, and then he offered her double what the part called for."

She stood very still, her thoughts turning to many occasions when she had seen Jordan display his "dog in the manger" complex, and suddenly she nodded and laughed.

"That checks," she admitted, and there was triumph as well as malice in her eyes as she looked at Martha. "Thanks, pet, for a perfectly swell idea. I think you've really given me an angle. If I can't do anything with it, then I don't deserve to win. 'Bye now."

She went briskly out and the door closed behind her.

CHAPTER FOURTEEN
RECIPE FOR A PARTY

JORDAN CALLED HER several times daily and there were daily offerings of flowers, usually with some gift enclosed. But she did not see him for four days. She knew that he was very busy whipping the new show into shape, and she was honestly relieved when the days slid by and he did not come to call. She was bitterly lonely, but now that she had faced and admitted that she loved Paul Whitney with all her heart, now that she had ceased to try to deceive herself about that, she knew that she would always be lonely without him, and so she might as well make the best of it. The thing for her to do, she told herself in the dreary, lonely watches of the night, was to go back to nursing. It was the one thing that could absorb her interest and she was anxious to get on with her training.

Jordan called near the end of her first week back in town, when he said gaily, "Do yourself up all pretty in your very best clothes, baby. You're going steppin' tonight."

"Am I?" she asked, and could not keep the eagerness out of her voice. "That sounds like fun."

"It will be, baby, it will be," said Jordan happily, obviously pleased by her eagerness. "We'll have dinner together, just the two of us, and then we'll drop in on Lisbeth's party for a while, and after that, anywhere you want to go, anything you want to do. I've got a free evening."

"Lisbeth's party?" Martha asked sharply.

"Sure. Decent of her, isn't it? But then she's been very decent about the whole business," said Jordan. And though he spoke with suitable seriousness, there was a hint of pride in his voice that two lovely women could be fighting over him. Because in what Martha now knew was his overweening egotism, that was the way it would seem to him. "I'll tell you all about it when I see you. Be there by seven."

Martha was justifiably uneasy and suspicious, because she knew perfectly well that Lisbeth had no intention of letting Jordan go back to his wife without a battle. Though just what Lisbeth could do, if Jordan wanted Martha instead of Lisbeth, Martha couldn't quite see. But she knew perfectly well that Lisbeth was a clever and a devious woman. She would stop at nothing. She had broadcast among her friends the fact that Martha was divorcing Jordan; she had made no secret of the fact that she expected to marry Jordan once the divorce was granted; and she wouldn't face without a fight the humilating necessity of admitting that she had lost out to Jordan's wife.

Still, Martha told herself over and over again, she couldn't quite see just what Lisbeth could do. Yet she dressed that night more carefully than she had ever dressed in her life, and when she had finished, and eyed herself in the mirror, she nodded in satisfaction. At least she would be armed with the knowledge that she was young and lovely and desirable, and nothing equips a woman for a battle with another woman like such knowledge.

Jordan stared at her when he came into the room, and his eyes flamed and she saw the hard-caught breath that shook him.

"How I ever let you get away from me, Martie—" he said at last in a tone sharp with wonder for all the softness of the voice in which he spoke.

Martha was a little frightened of the look in his eyes, but she made a gay little gesture of dismissal and laughed.

"Oh, I didn't know how to dress, and I was pretty 'green'," she told him lightly. "I've grown up now."

His eyes crept over her, and she saw the tip of his tongue touch his lips as he said softly, "You have, Martie; you certainly have."

He took a step toward her, but she evaded him gaily, and shook her head.

"You mustn't muss me, Jordy—it's taken me hours to accomplish this—this picture! And besides, I'm starving," she told him with a gaiety that was not quite convincing.

"So am I, Martie, and I'm not a patient man," he told her grimly.

"I warned you, Jordy, you'd much better just let me go." She could not quite keep the plea out of her voice, but Jordan's jaw only set more firmly, and he lifted her wrap.

"Shall we go?" he said icily.

And Martha lifted her shoulders in a little shrug of defeat

The moment they stepped into the apartment where Lisbeth was giving her party, Martha understood the reason for it. For from the two shallow steps that led down to the vast living room, the first person she saw was Paul.

Jordan was exchanging gaily insulting greetings with a group that had come in behind them, and for a moment Martha was free of his attention. Which was just as well, for she stood perfectly still, her hands clenched tightly, and her eyes wide and almost frightened, fastened on Paul's face. And across the long room, Paul looked at her, and lifted his cocktail in a little gesture like a toast, and Lisbeth claimed him.

Martha, across the length of the room, naturally could not hear, above the gay clamor of the party, what was said. But she could not miss, nor was she supposed to miss, the possessive little movement with which Lisbeth slipped her hand through Paul's arm, drew his hand down so that she could taste his cocktail, and then looked across the room straight at Martha with a mocking, triumphant smile.

The whole thing lasted barely a minute, the minute during which Jordan was greeting the group behind them. It ended when Jordan put a proprietary arm about her, and turned her to face the group, saying proudly, "You have been denied, up to now, a very great privilege. You haven't met my wife. Darling, these are some cherished enemies of mine."

Martha went through all the required motions of acknowledging the introductions, smiling, being pleasant and friendly; she went off with the other two women in the group to dispose of her wraps, and to touch up her makeup a little.

Martha was grateful for the knowledge that Paul was there, because when Lisbeth brought her and Jordan to where Paul stood, she could look up at him quietly, composedly, and smile faintly. If she had faced him without having caught that glimpse of him first...

"Paul, these are friends of mine," Lisbeth began gaily.

"Thanks," Jordan cut in grimly, his eyes meeting Paul's straightly, bitter enmity flashing between the two men like the flash of a naked sword. "We've met."

"We have indeed," said Paul dryly. "How are you, Ainslee?"

Lisbeth said gaily, "Oh, well, then, if you know each other. Paul, take good care of Martha while I take Jordan around and see that everybody meets him; he's the top celebrity of the evening."

They moved off together, and Paul and Martha were alone.

For a moment they stood very still, looking at each other without speech. And Martha had no way of knowing how much of her tremulous heart was in her eyes. Paul, as though drowned in her gaze, just stared. Then at last he spoke, his voice husky, deep-toned, reaching no farther than her ears.

"Hello, Martie," he said very softly.

"Hello, Paul," said Martha, and tore her eyes away from him with an effort that was almost physical and looked about the big room. "It looks like a good party."

"It's a lousy party, Martie, and we both know it, so why do we stay? Martie, how are you?"

"Why, I'm fine, Paul," she told him coolly. "I'm just perfectly fine." Her voice stumbled and she set her teeth hard.

He drew her into a corner beside the window where there was a semblance of privacy, and looked down at her gravely.

"You are looking more beautiful than ever, Martha," he admitted softly. "But what I want to know is, how are you *really?*"

"I just told you; I'm fine."

"Happy?"

Her smile was faint and too mature for her years.

"Deliriously—why wouldn't I be? Don't I have everything in the world any woman could ask for? Money, clothes, youth, a certain amount of good looks, and an adoring husband." Her voice faded a little on the last words, and Paul's hands clenched until he thrust them into his pockets as though he could not trust them.

"That, of course, is what I really wanted to know about, Martie—you and Jordan. Are things all right?" he asked harshly.

"Of course," said Martha brightly. Too brightly.

"Yet you're living apart?"

"He's terribly busy just now, putting a show together. The apartment—his apartment—is a madhouse." She broke off, drew a deep hard breath and lifted her chin. "And now is my turn to ask questions. How are you—and Lisbeth?"

Paul frowned a little and his jaw set.

"I'm fine; I wouldn't know about Lisbeth," he began.

"Oh, but now that Jordan has me, there is no reason why you can't have Lisbeth," she assured him lightly.

Paul stared at her, frowning.

"Well, I suppose not, provided I happened to want Lisbeth, which I don't, and provided she happened to want me, which isn't very likely," he said at last.

Martha made herself laugh at him, though her eyes were dark.

"Oh, now, you're just being proud and haughty," she said mockingly. "I was pretty stupid at first—I'm afraid I'm a pretty stupid person, after all. But I realized pretty soon, when I sort of woke up, that all you had done from the very beginning was so that you could have Lisbeth back."

Paul's brows had drawn together in a frown that was not only puzzled but a little angry.

"I suppose you have some small idea of what you're talking about?" he suggested at last.

"Well, of course."

"Good! Then maybe you'll explain it so I can understand."

"It's very simple, though it took me a long time to realize," she said clearly. "I was silly enough to think that you liked me a little, for myself, and then I realized that what you were really trying to do was break up my plans for a divorce so that Jordy couldn't marry Lisbeth, and then she'd come back to you."

Paul's jaw set in savage fury and his eyes blazed. But he was sufficiently aware of the gay, laughing clamorous groups about them to keep his voice low, despite his anger.

"That's very flattering," he said grimly, and he was hoarse with the effort to control himself. "That I'd go to such extremes to get Lisbeth, or any woman back. You have a very high opinion of me, haven't you?"

Martha lifted her eyes to his and looked straight at him.

"Yes, Paul, I have," she told him simply.

For a long moment Paul looked deeply into her eyes, and the anger went out of him and a fire flickered there that for a moment bathed her in its lovely glow. She had the oddest feeling that she had come in out of darkness and cold to a warm, fire-lit room.

"Darling," said Paul very low, his voice shaken, "don't you know yet—" He bit off the words, and the effort was one that tightened his jaw again. Then he looked across the room to where Jordan stood, as always the center of an admiring group, made up chiefly of the youngest and prettiest women in the room.

There was a taut moment of silence between them while her heart seemed to slow its beat in an almost unbearable suspense. And then Paul looked back at her and the lovely fire was gone from his eyes.

"So you and Ainslee have given up the idea of a divorce," he said dryly at last. "Yet you aren't sharing quarters."

"We're not living together," said Martha steadily. "He begged me for another chance; he's promised not to expect me to be his wife until I am in love with him again. But I won't ever be, Paul. I know it!"

There was such utter, such sober conviction in her tone that Paul asked curiously, frowning a little, "Then why do you string him along, Martie? Why do you let him keep hoping? That's neither kind nor sensible."

Martha spread her hands in a little hopeless gesture.

"I've told him and told him, Paul, but he simply can't believe there is any woman in the world who doesn't want him," she said simply, childishly. "He thinks I loved him once."

Paul asked sharply, "And you didn't?"

She shook her head, and there were tears in her eyes.

"No, Paul, I was in love with being loved, I suppose," she confessed Humbly. "I'd never known anybody like Jordy and I let myself be swept off my feet. And when he and Lisbeth threw me out, I thought my heart was broken. Wasn't I a silly fool? But that was because I hadn't met you yet."

For the space of a handful of heartbeats, Paul stood very still looking down at her, his eyes touched with that fire that had so warmed and thrilled her.

"Do you realize what you're saying?" he asked huskily at last.

Her smile was faint, warm, very sweet, and her eyes met his steadily.

"Of course," she told him simply. "I'm saying that I love *you*, not Jordy. That I never loved Jordy. But you mustn't let that make any difference to you, Paul, I know you're not in love with me."

Paul gave a little groan and said huskily, "Will you shut up? Of all the places in the world to tell a man that. Martie, I'm dying to take you in my arms and kiss the livin' daylights out of you!"

An eager, incredulous delight blazed for a moment in her eyes, and she held her breath as though she dared not breathe lest this magic moment of enchantment be destroyed forever.

"Paul!" she whispered faintly, in a tone of wonder and awe.

"You blessed little idiot!" said Paul thickly. "Didn't you know?"

"How could I? You made love to me, and then you walked out on me, and you sort of threw me back at Jordy," she stammered.

"And why, except that you'd told me you loved him and that you wanted him back? I thought you let me love you just because you were missing him so much, wanting him, needing him."

Her eyes were wide and round with astonishment.

"Oh, Paul, what a couple of fools we've been!" she stammered. "And all the time I thought you were just trying to send me back to Jordy so you could have Lisbeth!"

Paul grinned at her, but without mirth.

"We were a couple of fools, Martie, but we're not going to be any more!" he told her firmly. "You skip home and pack and beat it back to Pine Hill and reinstate that divorce proceeding —you hear me?"

"Oh, Paul!"

"And this time, don't hang around en route!" he ordered her tenderly, with make-believe sternness. "When Beelzy telephoned me you were taking off for Florida, I reached the station just ahead of you and I was right behind you in the line when you bought your ticket. Remember the clerk wasn't sure there was such a place and had to look it up and found you couldn't go there on the train? That you had to buy a ticket to Jacksonville, and then take the bus from there?"

She stared at him, wide-eyed.

"But, Paul, why were you interested? I mean, we'd never met or anything," she asked, puzzled.

Paul grinned ruefully.

"I'd seen you around with Jordy, and I knew Lisbeth," he said dryly, and added quietly, "I'm not going to begin by lying to you, Martie. I did have an affair with Lisbeth, and she ended it by taking up with Jordy, and you looked such a downy little day-old baby chick I felt you needed help. So I followed you to Pine Hill to keep an eye on you, and see if there was any way I could help you even the score with Jordan and Lisbeth."

"But when I got to Pine Hill you were already there," she puzzled.

He grinned at that.

"It's very simple—I flew!" he pointed out. "I landed the morning after you left New York. I was already established as a good-for-nothin' beach-combin' shell collector when you got there, which made it easy for me to keep an eye on you."

Martha drew a long, shaken breath and her eyes were eager.

"And from the moment I knew who you were, that night at Miami Beach, I've been sure as anything that everything you did was so you could get Lisbeth back!" she marveled.

"It was so that you could have a chance to make up your mind, Martie. You said you wanted Jordan. I loved you then as I love you now, enough to want you to have what *you* want, whatever it takes to make you happy. That night—Martie, you remember the night I mean?"

A lovely rose color flooded upward from throat to brow; her eyes met his steadily, and her smile was soft, sweet, tremulous.

"The night I came alive because at last I knew what love really was? Paul, I couldn't ever forget—not ever!" she told him shakily. "And next morning when you practically threw me out of your cabin—oh, Paul, if you loved me, how could you?"

"Because I loved you, darling, and because I didn't want you to make any mistake. You had said over and over that you loved Jordan, and I felt you were using me to appease your hunger for him, and I didn't want you to take me as second best and then some day regret it," he told her simply and straightforwardly.

For a long moment she looked up at him, wide-eyed, shaken.

"Oh, darling," she whispered huskily, her eyes misty. "If only you had told me then."

"But I couldn't be sure until you had seen Jordan again, don't you understand, sweet?" he pleaded.

"Yes, of course," she admitted. "But we've lost so much time."

"We'll make up for it, dearest, I promise you!" he told her softly. "Beginning tomorrow."

Startled, they realized suddenly that they were no longer alone. And when Martha turned, shaken, Jordan stood so close that he must have heard something of what they had been saying.

"If you're trying to wangle a commission to paint my lovely wife, Whitney, you're wasting your time," said Jordan, and his very tone was insulting. "When she sits for her portrait it will be for someone far more important in the art world than you."

"Jordy, you're insulting," protested Lisbeth hotly, her eyes spitting venom at Martha.

"Only a very great artist, which I am not nor ever claimed to be, could hope to do justice to Martie, Ainslee, so I feel you're quite right," said Paul. And Martha felt a little throb of pride in her heart because Paul was dismissing the whole thing in a casual manner that avoided unpleasantness, and she knew that it was for her sake.

For a moment they smiled at each other, and then Jordan drew Martha away to introduce her to some people who had just arrived, and a few minutes later Paul left the party. And with him, for Martha, went all the happiness and the glory of a beautiful new hope just born in her heart.

Jordan said bitingly in her ear, "You might at least have the decency to hide your lust for him *a* little, here in public."

Martha caught her breath and glanced up at him fearfully. But her voice was steady.

"I love him, Jordan. We might as well face it," she said quietly.

"Do you, now?" said Jordan politely as though his were a purely academic interest, but his jaw hardened until a little muscle leaped along it. "And no doubt he returns your tender affection? How could he not, you're so beautiful?"

"He loves me, Jordy, and tomorrow I'm leaving for Pine Hill." she told him steadily.

"Oh, now really." His tone was mocking, insolent, "Do have a little originality—there are other places in Florida."

"I know," she told him contentedly, her eyes touched with memories whose warmth made his eyes flicker a little. "But I like Pine Hill."

Jordan studied her with a little curious smile that she was too happy to notice, or to analyze if she had noticed.

"So I lose again, to Whitney!" he said after a moment. "It's getting to be a habit. As soon as I finish with a woman she crawls right into Whitney's bed. Maybe I should make an arrangement for some remuneration from him. After all the time I put in training women for him—"

But Martha, her head high, had walked away from him. For a little he stood quite still, watching her, until Lisbeth came close and claimed him, and he smiled down at her, his manner casual and gay and friendly. But the look in his eyes was still ugly.

CHAPTER FIFTEEN
HONEYMOON COTTAGE

IT WAS AN hour or so later that jordan came to where Martha was the center of a pleasant little group, reached down and took her hand and drew her to her feet.

"I'm taking my wife home, all you nice people," he said lightly, and Martha thought that only she caught the slight emphasis on "my wife." "It's been a lot of fun, Lisbeth. You must come up and see us sometime."

Martha quickly said her good-bys and went into the bedroom to collect her wrap.

When she came out Jordan was waiting for her, and his manner was gaily loverlike and devoted as they said their goodnights and went out to the elevator, and across the lobby toward the street.

Jordan's car sood at the curb a little way down the street, but there was no sign of Beelzy, and Jordan shrugged, tucked Martha into the front seat and said casually, "Oh, well, I'll drive you home, and then Beelzy can take a taxi. Serves him right for leaving the car unguarded."

"He's probably having a drink," Martha began.

"Beelzy doesn't drink," said Jordan, and slid himself beneath the wheel. "Isn't that a laugh? Still keeps himself in condition— for what I wouldn't know."

He had drawn a bunch of keys from his pocket, selected the right one and started the car. As it swung away from the curb, he said lightly, "Look at that moon, Martha—or can you? It looks lost in this huge sprawling madhouse of a town, doesn't it? Let's go for a little drive, Martie, and see what a moon looks like away from all these cockeyed electric lights."

"Oh, but it's late, Jordy."

"So it's late," agreed Jordan like a stubborn child. "So what? You can sleep the clock around if you like, and I can always do with a couple of hours sleep and get up fresh as a daisy—to coin a phrase. Be a sport, Martie."

"All right," said Martha, laughing a little and relaxing. "But when Beelzy finds the car gone, and takes a taxi home and you're not there, he'll probably sound a general alarm and start hunting you like crazy."

"You don't like Beelzy, do you, Martie?" asked Jordan. As the car spurted ahead, a passing streetlight flung its dimness for a moment across his face and she saw that it was set and angry.

"Beelzy has never liked me, Jordy," she said quietly. "But he's devoted to you, and I've tried to like him for that."

"How touching!" said Jordan dryly. "Especially as you dislike me even more than you dislike him."

Martha tensed a little, but his tone was quietly grave, and his face, in the dim light from the instrument board, was expressionless.

"That's not true, Jordy," she said quietly. "I don't dislike you. I owe you a great deal, in a great many ways, and I'm grateful. But I'm sorry, Jordy, that I don't love you."

"Naturally not. Now that you know Paul Whitney, the Great Lover, how could you possibly care for a dope like me?"

"I did love you, Jordy."

His little exclamation was a derisive oath.

"But you didn't exactly do anything to keep me in love with you, did you? You were unfaithful to me within two weeks, maybe less, of our marriage."

"You were such a little innocent."

"Wasn't that something you should have taken care of? You wouldn't have wanted me to marry you if I'd been trained to love by half a dozen different lovers, would you?" she asked through her teeth.

"I really don't know—I suppose not," he agreed, and seemed to think the subject had been exhausted.

They drove for a little in silence. The car moved almost without sound but at a speed that frightened Martha, though she knew Jordan was an expert driver, and that while he had been drinking, he was in no way drunk. And to protest the speed might add to the fuel of his slow-burning anger that her instinct told her was building up in him.

At last she roused herself enough to say lightly, "Goodness, we really are in the country, aren't we? Where are we, Jordy?"

"Long Island," he said curtly.

"Well, don't you think it's time we turned back?" asked Martha uneasily.

"Why should we? I'm in no hurry. Do you have a late date with Paul?" he drawled, his tone an insult deeper than the implication in the words.

"Of course not."

"Not very enterprising of him," said Jordan carelessly. "He could have had you right there before the whole party if he had wanted you—your attitude toward him made that disgustingly plain."

Martha gasped as though he had slapped her and her hands tightened in her lap. But she would not give him the satisfaction of quarreling with him. A small, creeping fear that was like a cold, tiny snake was beginning to move in her heart. She tried to deny that she was afraid of Jordan. And yet how well did she know him? She was appalled to realize that though she was married to this man, though she had lived with him as his wife for a brief interval, she scarcely knew him at all. And she had first met him as a patient in a "mental hospital." She barely managed not to shiver. Jordan looked down at her as though he had read her thoughts, and in the dim light from the instrument panel his eyes were shining.

"Cold?" he asked solicitously. "We're almost there—just around that curve in the road."

Martha became newly conscious of her surroundings, and was startled to discover that they had left the main highway for a secondary road, which they were now leaving to follow a sandy, winding road almost narrow enough to be called a lane. The big car was having some difficulty in negotiating the road's sharp curves.

She sat up and stared, and now that tiny snake of fear had grown to king size and she felt as though its coils wrapped her whole body and sent it shivering.

"Jordan, where are we? Where are we going? We must be miles from anywhere!" she stammered, trying desperately to steady her voice so that he would not suspect how frightened she was.

"Our honeymoon cottage, sweet." Jordan's voice was mocking, derisive. "I thought it would be nice if we had an old-fashioned honeymoon away from it all. We didn't have anything that could be called a proper honeymoon before, so when I knew you were coming back to me—"

"I'm not, Jordy, I'm not!"

"I looked around," he went on as though she had not spoken, "and stumbled on this cottage. You're going to love it—just the place an innocent little country gal like you would like. Only five rooms, and the nearest neighbor a mile away. Just you and me, sweet, all alone here, with the sun and the sand and the stars— wonderful, isn't it?"

He was laughing soundlessly, and there was a tone in his voice that terrified her. But she fought for her self-control, sensing somehow that she mustn't let him know she was frightened.

"That was sweet of you. Jordy." She made her voice gentle and held it as steady as she could as she laid a hand on his arm. "But, Jordy, it's too late. Please take me back to town."

"Oh, but not until you've seen the cottage—you wouldn't be so unkind as not even to look at the place I bought and furnished just as a shrine for our great happiness?" said Jordan, and though the words were pleasant enough his tone made them an ugly mockery.

They had driven around the curve in the road now and the cottage lay before them. A small white cottage, with wide deep windows, shuttered in green. It faced the Sound, and the beach that was silvery-white in the moonlight.

Jordan stopped the car and jumped out.

"Come on, Martie, and look at it. And then I'll drive you home. I promise!"

Humor him, Martie! Humor him! her frantic mind urged her.

"Of course, Jordy—it's a darling house," she said with an attempt at gaiety that was completely unconvincing in her own ears.

Jordan fitted a key into the lock, turned the knob and pushed open the door. He fumbled inside, found an electric switch, and amber light bloomed from several shaded lamps scattered about the enormous living room that seemed to comprise almost half of the house.

It really was charming, and for just a moment, in her delight at its charm, Martha forgot her fear. But before she could enter the house, Jordan had scooped her up in his arms and was carrying her across the threshold.

"We musn't ignore the ancient traditions, Martie, m'love," he said mockingly as he put her on her feet in the center of the room. "Not bad, do you think?"

Martha looked at pale blond wood, at beautifully patterned chintz and delicately colored flower prints and the shining floors, where an occasional hooked rug added its own note of color.

"Not bad? Jordy, it's lovely! It's charming! I love it," she told him quite sincerely.

Jordan studied her for a long moment, and then he chuckled dryly.

"Well, that's good, because you're going to be here for a long, long time," he told her casually, as he turned the key in the lock and put the key in his pocket. "By the time I'm ready for you to leave, I doubt if dear, dear Paul will be able to stand the sight of you."

Martha drew away from him, unable now to conceal her fear.

"Jordy, you don't know what you're saying," she panted.

Jordan chuckled deep in his throat, and the look in his eyes chilled her to the bone.

"Oh, yes, I know exactly what I'm saying," he told her coolly. "I'm saying that Whitney can have you when I've quite finished with you, provided he wants you then, which I seriously doubt. You're a lovely thing, Martie, and I've been a fool, almost letting you go. But you're here now, and there's no way out, because I'm a most efficent guard."

He was coming closer, and Martha, without realizing it, was retreating, her hands flung up, her face pallid, her eyes wide and sick.

"Jordy, you promised, you promised," she panted.

His mouth curled in an ugly grin that was more than half a sneer.

"I did, didn't I?" he admitted as though he found that unpleasantly amusing. "And wasn't I the damned fool? To think I could be around you, wanting you like hell, and let you keep on brushing me off so that you could go to Whitney! What a laugh!"

She had retreated from him now until her back was against the wall and she could retreat no farther. She looked at him in sick panic, her pleading dying on her lips beneath the look of his dark, congested face, knowing before she spoke the utter uselessness of any pleading.

His hands reached for her and grasped her. She shrank between his hands, and felt the soft, silken sound of caramel-colored lace and chiffon as it tore. His hands, shaking a little now, ripped away the last vestige of her fragile garments, and his eyes blazing, he lifted her in his arms. She fought him, but his strength made mockery of her efforts, and Martha sank into a black, evil pit....

Afterwards, when the savage emotion that had driven him like an inhuman goad had died down, he looked down at her where she lay huddled, her face hidden against the pillow.

"Next time don't fight me," he said through his teeth. "It'll go much easier with you. The sooner you admit that you belong to me just as much as a horse or other beast I have bought and paid for, the easier things will go with you."

Dazed, uncomprehending, scarcely able to believe that he was really saying this, she lifted her tear-drenched face and stared at him incredulously.

"You—you're mad!" she whispered, sick with horror and shame. "You're stark, staring mad!"

For a moment an expression unlike anything she had ever seen on his face before flickered across it. There was for a moment something like panic in his eyes and then he took a step toward her, menacingly.

"Don't say that, do you hear me? Don't ever say that again! Ever!" His voice was thick, husky, shaken.

Rashly, knowing that she had him at a point where it hurt, she cried out, "It's true and you know it. Dr. Litton was shocked when he found I wanted to marry you."

Jordan had himself under some measure of control now. His smile was thin and unpleasant.

"So was I," he drawled insolently. "Just because I made careless love to you in the back seat of my car, you instantly leaped to the conclusion that I wanted to marry you! I didn't—I never did. It was as Lisbeth said, a spite marriage—I married you to spite her!"

"Of course," said Martha unsteadily, and stood up, reaching for something with which to cover herself. Jordan, laughing, walked to a closet, flung open a door, and waved to its contents. "I had them packed and brought out here, since you didn't want to take them to Florida with you. Rather neat, don't you think? You take off for Florida with Whitney, refusing to take with you anything I paid for, but Whitney changed your mind quick about that, didn't he? He prefers you with a healthy settlement or a big chunk of alimony. Why else would he want to tie up with a wanton like you?"

She was clothing herself hastily, shrinking beneath his eyes as he smoked and watched her avidly. She felt that if she didn't get out of the place in another few minutes she would scream the place down. She turned toward the door, fastening her blouse as she went, and managed to evade Jordan's outstretched hand. But before she could reach the front door and escape, Jordan had lunged after her and caught her.

He laughed a little as he held her, and when she sobbed that he was hurting her his grip only grew more painful, and his smile more awful. Through the haze of pain and shock that shook her, she heard dimly somewhere the sound of a door opening. It was a gentle sound, one that undoubtedly Jordan; dark desire sweeping him again at the touch of her warm, struggling body in his arms, did not hear.

Then suddenly across his shoulder, she saw the door to the kitchen open and gave a little sobbing cry of relief as she recognized Beelzy.

"Leave go o' her, boss; you're hurtin' her," said Beelzy softly.

"You keep out of this, Beelzy," Jordan gritted savagely. "Get the hell out of here."

"I said leave go of her, boss, an' I meant it," said Beelzy as Martha whimpered.

Jordan turned his head, and Beelzy drew back his hamlike fist and drove it straight at Jordan's chin. There was an ugly, meaty smacking sound as the fist connected, and Jordan looked dazed and his arms loosened, and he went backward to fall sprawling on his back.

He was very still, and Beelzy stood staring down at him absently massaging his fist with his sound hand, and swearing under his breath.

"I konked the boss!" he said at last in a tone of awe and shock and grief. "Me, Beelzy—I konked the boss!"

"Oh, Beelzy, thank you," stammered Martha.

Beelzy whirled on her as though just remembering for the first time that she was here.

"Why the hell didn't you sock him?" he barked at her furiously. "Where was all that classy judo you're so proud of?"

Martha stared at him, round-eyed.

"Judo?" she repeated as though she had never before in her life heard the word. "I—Beelzy, I never thought of it."

Once more Beelzy swore that slow, steady stream of purple oaths, and when she could understand him again he was saying savagely, "You never thought of it! Your old man knocks himself out teaching you judo; you throw it around like crazy when it ain't needed—when you ain't got no call to use it—but when you get up against a jam like this, you never thought of it. And it's gotta be me that comes along and konks the boss, and he ain't ever gonna forget it, neither."

"Beelzy, I'm sorry."

"Sorry—smorry—hell!" Beelzy had knelt beside Jordan, and assured himself that he was merely knocked out, not dead. And then he rose and stood over his employer as though defending him, and his ugly face was livid with fury. "What kind of dame are you, anyhow? Sleep with the boss a few times, get him crazy for you. then beat the hell out with some other guy and tell the boss you want a divorce. Then when he comes to fix things up so you can have it, you don' want a divorce after all, and you come back to town with him—but you won't sleep with him any more, though you know he's damned near crazy from wanting you to. And then you come off out here with him to this dump, and when he takes for granted the reason you come, like any guy would, you go all coy on him, and get in a fight with him an' I gotta slug him. What the hell are you trying to do, drive him nuts? Well, take a good look, sister; looks like you've made it."

Martha drew an uneven breath and her hands were clenched tightly.

"You—you mean he is mentally ill?" she stammered faintly.

Beelzy's ugly face twisted malevolently.

"No, I don't mean he's 'mentally ill'," he mimicked her tone. "I mean he's what the flap-jaws in the flossy medical joints call a 'borderline' case. Things go nice and smooth for him, he'll be all okay; but if he runs into something like this—frustration, the doc said was tough for him—and if this ain't frustration then all them books I been readin' since he was 'took' is liars."

"I didn't know, Beelzy."

"Well, we wasn't exactly standin' on street corners yacking it to the whole damned world," snapped Beelzy. "A guy'd think a jane like you that'd worked in one of them nut-factories would have a little sense. Either take him or leave him be; don't try to do both. And now get the hell out and lemme look after the boss. Go on—beat it."

"I—Beelzy, I don't even know where I am, or how to get back to town."

Beelzy swore under his breath.

"I waited home for the boss until I was sure he wasn't comin' and then I asked the doorman of the Harlow dame's apartment and he said you and the boss drove off together while I was snaggin' a glass o' milk. I went on home, and when he didn't show, I got the guy at your joint and he said you hadn't come in; then I thought o' this dump. I had a hunch you'd come here, so I hopped a taxi and had him bring me out. He's a pal o' mine and he's waiting down the road a piece for me. Tell him I said to take you home. And stay out o' the boss's way from now on, or s'help me, I'll bat your brains out—me, myself, personally!"

Martha said humbly. "Will he—Beelzy, will he be all right?"

"Oh, sure, sure," snarled Beelzy savagely. "He'll be just dandy. He'll probably wind up in some exclusive nut-hatchery cuttin' out paper dolls and talkin' to hisself, like his old man done. I spent many a year trying to ride herd on the boss and keep him from windin' up like that, but—aw, hell, beat it! D'you hear? Scramola, but fast!"

"Yes, Beelzy," said Martha faintly, and stumbled out of the house into the glory of the newborn day.

CHAPTER SIXTEEN
SOME MEDICAL ADVICE

THE TAXI DRIVER looked distinctly uneasy as she came almost running down the narrow twisting road and tumbled into the taxi. But he nodded when she told him that Beelzy would stay with his boss, and drive him back to town.

Martha tried to pull herself together, knowing that the taxi driver was watching her covertly through the rear-vision mirror, and when she stepped out of the taxi in front of her apartment house, she said hurriedly to the doorman, "Give my taxi driver ten dollars, John. I'll send it down to you as soon as I get upstairs."

"Of course, Mrs. Ainslee, it's a pleasure," said John ceremoniously. But as she reached the steps, she heard the two men laugh and her ears burned.

She reached her apartment with the feeling of having reached sanctuary at long last. A place where she could lock the door and be alone and safe! For the first time she had the opportunity to sit down, to realize, to face the ugliness of what had happened. To draw a deep breath and, shuddering, look back.

She would never be able to face Jordan, or even to think of him, without a sick loathing and disgust. The brutality of his attack—for it had been that, nothing less—had shaken her to the very depths of her being. She had never known that anything could be so horrible, and now even the thought of Paul was ugly and repulsive to her. She shrank from the thought that Paul wanted her as Jordan did, and suddenly she was on her feet, once more the instinct for mad, thoughtless flight taking possession of her. She had to get away; away from both men who wanted her. She had to lose the feeling of being a bone between two dogs who fought savagely to possess her. And she was too wrought up, too overcharged to stop and face sanely the fact that Paul had never been anything but gentle, that Paul loved her. All she could grasp now was that Paul wanted her—and she could endure no more of such thought.

Even as she flung a few things into a suitcase, her mind sought frantically for some harbor where she could be safe, and like a drink of cooling water to one parched of thirst in the desert, it came to her: Home! Home! The aunts, loving, gentle, unquestioning, would welcome her warmly. And her breath came in a little sob of passionate thanksgiving that they would be there waiting for her, welcoming her, loving her. And there was her nursing. Maybe she could go back in training right away.

But even as she finished her brief preparations she knew that Paul would come for her soon; that any moment the telephone might ring and his voice would speak in her ear. She had promised she would go back to Pine Hill with him and he would have to have some explanation of her unwillingness to do so. Instinctively she knew that she must not tell Paul about Jordan; there would be trouble between the two men, and she was sick of trouble.

She wrote swiftly:

"Dear Paul,
   I'm going home for a few days. I have to have time to think things out. I'll write to you soon.
                                        Martha."

She hesitated a moment, almost wrote "I love you" and stayed her hand. For in this moment of mental chaos and pain and confusion, she couldn't be sure even of that. She sealed the note in an envelope, scrawled his name across it and went down to the lobby, carrying her overnight case, all the baggage she meant to burden herself with.

She left the note at the desk to be given to Paul when he called to take her to lunch. Outside, she gave John the ten dollars to repay him for what he had paid the taxi driver. And inside the cab that John whistled up, she examined the contents of her purse. A lone five-dollar bill, two ones and some change. Her mouth twisted a little wryly, and she shrugged. It was enough to get her back home to Aunt Elizabeth and Aunt Arleen, and after that—well, after that was time enough to worry. ...

She was like a homesick child when she came up the walk and saw with eyes blurred with tears the dear familiar outline of the shabby old house. And when, in answer to her knock, Aunt Elizabeth opened the door, Martha hurled herself in the outstretched arms and burst into tears.

The two old women hovered about her, anxious-eyed, their voices warm and soothing, as they asked no questions but waited for her paroxysms of tears to be finished before she told them why she was at home. She would tell them all in her own good time, they reasoned peacefully.

She finished with weeping at last, put down the tea Aunt Arleen had brought her, and said huskily, "You're so good to me. You're good for me."

"Oh, fiddlesticks," said Aunt Elizabeth, and brushed that aside. "We're just so glad to see you, Martie. It's been such a long time. And so much has happened to you, but we're not going to talk about that now. You're worn out, and you're going upstairs and have a nice nap, and we'll talk later."

"That sounds like heaven," said Martha gratefully.

She let them help her out of her clothes, into a nightgown, and then crept into bed. She wouldn't sleep, of course, she told herself, but she would rest. She was so desperately tired—and knew no more until dusk filled the room and downstairs she could hear the subdued murmur of voices and faint tinkling sounds that told her the aunts were getting dinner ready.

She yawned and stretched luxuriously, and winced a little as memory came back, but she had faced and turned away from the worst of her troubles in the long, dreamless sleep. And she would look ahead, not back—which was all very easy to say but not too easy to do.

She got up, dressed in one of the shabby, beloved gingham dresses she had left behind and went down to dinner.

The kichen looked strange and alien to her at first sight and she paused, startled, in the doorway; the aunts were busy and for a moment did not see her. After her marriage, she had bought them a new electric ice box and freezer and washing machine; she had had the kitchen wired for an electric stove and had bought the finest one for them she could find. And now, looking at the quaint old room, she blushed a little, for the gleaming white intruders looked painfully out of place there with the well-remembered crisp red and white scrim curtains at the windows, with the inevitable row of Aunt Elizabeth's cherished pot-plants blooming luxuriously. The new linoleum, the new equipment seemed to sneer haughtily at the well-scrubbed old kitchen table. The new equipment, she told herself wryly, was like herself—out of place. She belonged here in this worn, tidy, neat kitchen, in this shabby old house, among people who shared her sense of values, who believed in the things she had been brought up to believe in. The fancy, expensive new equipment had intruded, just as Jordan had intruded on her life.

But before she could pursue the thought to its logical conclusion, Aunt Elizabeth turned and saw her, and greeted her with loving warmth, and Arleen, busily basting the roasting duckling, smiled over her shoulder, and everything became peaceful and warm and ordinary.

At the table, Martha said quietly, "I've made an awful mess of things, darlings, and I'll tell you a little about it, but then, if you don't mind, I'd rather not talk about it."

"You don't even have to tell us a little about it, child," said Aunt Elizabeth firmly. "We know you; we raised you; we know that if you are in trouble, it is not your fault. And that's all we need to know."

Martha stared at her through a blur of tears.

"Darling, you're wonderful!" she said thickly. "But I want you to know. I wrote you that I had gone to Florida to get a divorce from Jordan."

Aunt Arleen said firmly, "We thought you were quite wise."

Martha smothered a small, ashamed chuckle.

"What did you think when I wrote you I'd changed my mind and come back with him to New York?" she asked sheepishly.

Aunt Elizabeth hesitated and then she said quietly, "We felt you were being foolish, Martie, but that you were sort of leaning over backward to give him a second chance. And now that you've come home this way, we have sense enough to realize that you've found it wouldn't work and that you are going ahead with your plans for a divorce."

Martha looked down at her plate and her hands were clenched tightly in her lap.

"You're quite right, darling," she said huskily. "I know how you both feel about divorce."

"I wonder if you do," interrupted Aunt Arleen quietly.

Martha looked up at her swiftly.

"We have expected this, darling, since the day you eloped with Jordan," Aunt Elizabeth explained gently. "We knew from the first that such a marriage wouldn't work. Not for a girl like you, Martie. You belong in different worlds, you and Jordan. He would never make any effort to live in your world—one could not expect it—and you could never be happy in his. Jordan's always had too much money, too little discipline; he's spoiled and selfish. I'm sorry, dear, but you know it is the truth. And you—well, you wouldn't want to become a nurse, Martie, if money were important enough to you to make you happy in a world like Jordan's.

So we knew it wouldn't last. And we have worried about you, because you're all we have, Martie, and we want your happiness above everything in the world."

Martha smiled at them through her tears and did not try for further words.

The next day she walked across the fields to Happy Valley and Dr. Litton. He was unaffectedly glad to see her, and if he was surprised at seeing her here, wearing the shabby old coat and skirt and sweater she had worn when she was a student nurse, he did not comment on it.

She wasted little time in preliminaries, because she knew that he was a busy man and that he was impatient of people who prowled around the outer edges of a problem, instead of laying it before him in as few words as possible.

"Dr. Litton, I have to ask you something terribly important," she told him flatly. "I have to ask you whether you think that my divorcing Jordan may send him over the borderline, destroy him mentally."

Ever afterward she remembered with warm gratitude the promptness with which Dr. Litton flung back his gray head and laughed. A laugh of honest, genuine amusement that set a twinkle alight in his eyes.

"My dear child!" His voice was a little teasing. "I hate to destroy your illusions, but I am afraid there are not too many men who can be so easily destroyed. Oh, I grant you a long period of nagging, quarreling, frustration, bitterness—provided a man is emotionally unbalanced to begin with—could have a disastrous effect. But not on a man like Jordan Ainslee. If ever I saw a man who was quite able to take a divorce in his stride, Ainslee is the man."

"No matter how much he might desire me?" Martha begged for double assurance.

Dr. Litton's eyes were no longer twinkling.

"No matter how much he might desire you, Martha," he said quietly. "Oh, I grant you that if you were with him constantly, teasing him, pretending to offer yourself, the results might not be too good. For Ainslee is not too emotionally stable. But if you go right away from him, leave him for good, stay out of his sight, get a divorce, remove yourself from his vicinity, I feel quite sure he will solace himself with some other pretty without the slightest harm to his mental welfare. That, of course, Martha, is the reason I was so opposed to your marrying him in the first place—only you wouldn't listen."

"I know; I was a stupid fool."

"No, Martie, you were young and in love with glamour, which Ainslee represented to you at the time," said Dr. Litton.

She hesitated for a moment, and then quietly, simply, she told him of Jordan's attack in the cottage on Long Island and of Beelzy's arrival and of what Beelzy had said. And Dr. Litton listened quietly, watching her strained young face, her eyes that could not quite meet his own, because it was an ugly and shameful story that she had to tell him. And when she had finished, he nodded.

"That doesn't alter my conviction in the least, Martha, that the wisest, kindest thing you can do for Ainslee is to take yourself right out of his life for good," he said then. "Coming back with him to New York, denying him his marital privileges while living under his protection, appearing publicly as his wife yet insisting on living privately as his—sister—that's not good, Martie. Marriage in name only is one of the silliest and most dangerous things any couple can attempt. No, Martie, get your divorce and find yourself a husband who shares your own interests and desires. One with whom you can have a normal, happy life, with children." He broke off as the hot color surged over Martha's face and for a moment she hid her face in her hands.

"I see," said Dr. Litton gravely. "There is another man."

Miserably, Martha nodded. "Only the very thought of—of—" She broke off and shuddered.

Dr. Litton said sternly, "Stop this foolishness, Martha! Just because Jordan was a brute doesn't mean that all men are. And he had almost sufficient provocation for excuse. Oh, don't look at me like that. Sex is by no means all of love, but it's a damned important part, and don't you pretend it isn't! This man you speak of—is he physically repugnant to you?"

"Not—not until after Jordan—" She broke off, stammering, looking fearfully at Dr. Litton, whose eyes sharpened a little.

"Oh," said Dr. Litton flatly. "You have already had sexual relations with this other man?"

Though asked in the form of a question, his tone made it a statement, and Martha nodded, still unable to meet his eyes.

"And was it fun?" asked Dr. Litton.

She gasped and her eyes flew wide and met his, and suddenly there was a little warm softness in her heart and she said very low. "It was wonderful."

"Better than with Jordan when you were first married?" asked Dr. Litton.

Scarlet-cheeked, but her eyes steady, she nodded.

"Does he want to marry you, this other man? Can he marry you, or is he already married?" he probed relentlessly.

"Oh, no, he's not married—he wants to marry me."

"And you?"

"Until that night with Jordy, I wanted it, too."

"Then for heaven's sake, what's all this whooptedoo about?" demanded Dr. Litton angrily. "You come here and take up my time yammering away, asking advice, and you know damned well all the time that you're going to marry this other man just as soon as you can divorce Jordan Ainslee, don't you?"

"I do now," she told him shakily.

"Well, I should damned well hope so!" snapped Dr. Litton. "And, Martha, forget all this about Ainslee; start all over again, fresh and new, and make a good marriage this time, promise me?"

Martha stood up and her eyes were warm and steady.

"I promise," she said. Dr. Litton nodded, smiled, and unexpectedly bent his handsome gray head and kissed her cheek lightly.

"That's for your father, my friend," he said, and patted her hand.

Martha went out and down across the fields, through the meadow, her hands jammed deeply into the pockets of her shabby old coat, the wind tugging at her hair, blowing it about her face, so that she was upon the man who rose from a low stump and stood in front of her almost before she saw him. She gave *a* start and shrank back a step and blinked, quite sure for a moment that she had merely been thinking of him so hard that her imagination had conjured up a vision of him there before her.

"Remember me? The name is Whitney," said Paul grimly, and his eyes were cold, his jaw set and hard.

"Paul!" she breathed, her voice so shaken that the sound of it reached barely to his ear.

He nodded, his grimness unrelenting.

"That's right, Paul Whitney. The guy you took for as nice a little buggy ride as any one could wish for." He was angry with her and he bit the words off short. "I suppose if I'd had ten cents' worth of pride, I'd have taken my 'brush-off' like a gentleman, but somehow I didn't seem to have much pride. But I had one hell of a lot of curiosity, so I came up, as soon as I could find out where 'home' was, to demand an explanation. It was, in case you are interested which you probably are not, Lisbeth who finally broke down and told me where you had lived with your aunts and where you probably considered yourself at home."

"Paul, Paul," she stammered, and now there were tears in her eyes and her clenched hands were shaking.

He frowned at her, puzzled now as well as angry.

"Don't just stand there yapping 'Paul, Paul.' I want to know why the infernal hell you gave me that song-and-dance at

Lisbeth's party and then ran out on me next morning. Come on, give!" he demanded savagely.

"Oh, Paul!"

He caught her by the shoulders and shook her, or tried to. But before he could do more than touch her, she was in his arms, clinging to him, weeping a little. For a moment his hungry arms sought her, and then, his jaw set and hard, he thrust her away from him.

"Come on, out with it—what had I done to make you run off?" he demanded, and now his own voice was a little shaken.

"It was nothing you'd done, Paul." She had managed now to speak. "It was Jordan."

"That doesn't make any sort of sense at all," he protested, more puzzled now than angry.

And so briefly, trying to soften the ugliness as much as she could, knowing that she had no right to conceal from him the truth, she told him of Jordan's behavior. And before she had finished, Paul was standing a little away from her, his hands jammed in his pockets, his face set.

"So to be sure I wouldn't treat you the same way, you took off like a bat out of hell," he said when she had finished. "Well, thanks. That's very flattering. But at least it explains a lot. Your opinion of me is interesting, to say the least of it. And the least of it is what I would prefer to say."

"So then I came home," she went on steadily as though he had not spoken, "and this morning I had a long talk with Dr. Litton and he says there is no danger that Jordan needs me to prevent his becoming mentally ill."

Paul looked startled at the implication, and Martha rushed on.

"Dr. Litton says the kindest thing I can do is get my divorce as quickly as possible, to set Jordan free and then stay out of his sight until he forgets me," she finished, and there was a stray dimple in her cheek as she added for good measure, "Dr. Litton didn't seem to think that would be more than a few hours."

"Dr. Litton sounds like a very wise old owl," said Paul grimly. "So now, under doctor's orders, you're going to get a divorce. What then?"

"I guess it seems a little silly after all this time, Paul, but I'm going back to nursing. I want to graduate and be an R.N. I think being a student nurse is wonderful training for any girl, anyway, and I've always wanted to finish. Jordan—well, Jordan and I were really world's apart. He was kind of an interlude. And I can't let an interruption change my career."

Paul looked a little downcast. "Is that your whole life plan? Isn't there anything else you want to do?"

She flashed a smile. "Well, I said I thought nursing is wonderful training for a girl. I mean, it kind of trains her for—for marriage. I *had* planned to be married again. But—I'm not sure my prospective bridegroom hasn't changed his mind since then."

"Oh? Is he likely to be that big a fool?" asked Paul.

"He's not a fool at all—he's wise and good and kind and gentle and sweet and pretty wonderful!" Her eyes were shining.

"Oh," said Paul, in a deflated tone. "For a moment I was hoping you meant me."

"You blessed idiot," said Martha unsteadily and this time when she stumbled into his arms, they caught her close and held her tightly.

After a long, long moment he said shakily, "Martha, do we have to go back to Pine Hill?"

Her heart contracted painfully for a moment, but she lifted her head and faced him straightly.

"Of course not, darling—I'll be your mistress," she began.

Scandalized, Paul kissed her to silence.

"Hush such hussy-talk! I only meant that divorces come faster in Nevada, and I think you'd like it out there."

"If you'll be there, I'll like it," said Martha radiantly, and lifted her mouth for his kiss.

After a while she drew away. "I'm glad, darling," she said.

He cocked an eyebrow at her. "About what?" he asked. "My dimples?"

"No. Don't be silly. I mean, I'm glad we're going to Nevada because—because it will be quick. And because I can go back to studying sooner that way. But, there's one thing. When I go back to nursing, we won't be able to see much of each other for a while."

Paul grinned. "We'll have to make the most of your days off," he said. He caught her up in his arms again, and pressed his lips to hers. Suddenly he pulled away. "Hey!" he said, "do you remember how the fire escapes work on those nurses' dormitories?"

www.ingramcontent.com/pod-product-compliance
Lightning Source LLC
Chambersburg PA
CBHW030347180626
46812CB00007B/2787